ISBN: 978 1 763733909

First Edition.

This is a work of fiction, first written in 2014. Names, characters, places, and incidents are either the product of the author's imagination or used fictitiously. Any resemblance to actual events, locales, or persons, living or dead, is entirely coincidental.

Cover Design by the author, P R Bird

Cover Art by Yulia Pavlova, Russia

Trigger warning: Explicit content, 18+ (NOT FOR YOUNGER READERS)

This book contains mature themes subject to domestic violence, sexual assault, physical abuse, psychological abuse, drug use, murder, animal cruelty, larceny, and suicidal ideation.

1

The sun had just dipped below the horizon, casting long shadows across the quiet suburban streets. The air was thick with the promise of a warm summer night, and the distant hum of cicadas filled the silence. Inside the Finch household, the atmosphere was anything but serene.

Anna sat at her desk; her room illuminated by the soft glow of her desk lamp. She was engrossed in her assignment, the pages of her textbook spread out before her. The sound of her sister's laughter echoed down the hallway, breaking her concentration. Charlotte's voice, high-pitched and excited, was a stark contrast to the quiet determination that filled Anna's room.

"Anna!" Charlotte's voice rang out, accompanied by the sound of her footsteps approaching. Anna sighed, knowing that her sister's presence usually meant trouble. She glanced at the clock on her desk; it was 8:30 PM. She had hoped to finish her work before any distractions arose.

Charlotte burst into the room, her face alight with excitement. "Guess what?" she exclaimed, waving her phone in front of Anna's face. "We've been invited to Colin's party tonight!"

Anna frowned, her mind still on her assignment. "I'm busy, Charlotte. I have an important assignment due."

Charlotte rolled her eyes dramatically. "Oh, come on, Anna. It's Friday night! You can't spend your whole life buried in books. Besides, Richard will be there."

At the mention of Richard, Anna's heart skipped a beat. Richard, her ex-boyfriend, the one she wasn't quite over. The one whose breakup had been orchestrated by none other than Charlotte herself. The thought of seeing him again was both thrilling and terrifying.

Anna hesitated, her resolve wavering. She looked at her sister, who was practically bouncing with anticipation. "Fine," she said finally, "but I want to be home by 11 PM."

Charlotte grinned triumphantly. "Deal. I'll be in the car."

As Charlotte disappeared down the hallway, Anna took a deep breath. She closed her textbook and stood up, a mix of excitement and dread churning in her stomach. Tonight, was going to be interesting, to say the least.

I am Anna Finch, and Charlotte is my older sister, though at times I suspect she might be the devil incarnate. I always knew she harboured a deep-seated hatred for me, but her reasons remained an enigma. In truth, I never comprehended her actions or motivations. The only certainty was that Charlotte had profound issues and chose to vent all her frustrations on me. Charlotte had always harboured a mean streak towards me. Even as young children, she would do and say things to upset me. Regardless of the situation, she always knew she could get away with it because our mother was never around to discipline her. Our father, perpetually lost in his own world, was too detached to care or even acknowledge us most of the time. Charlotte would hit me or break my belongings, and since Dad did absolutely nothing about it, I had to learn to accept and forget. Eventually, I stopped having nice things altogether and refused any gifts, knowing Charlotte would either take or destroy them. It is no wonder that, even from an early age, I was quite disheartened with life.

I recall when Charlotte and I were young, and every time a thunderstorm struck, she would climb into my bed in the middle of the night, terrified of the thunder and lightning. I didn't mind, although I probably should have, considering she was never kind to me. Occasionally, I would kick her out after a few hours; we were small, but even two children couldn't comfortably share a single bed. Had I known she would use me as a punching bag as we grew older, I would never have let her in my bed or comforted her when she was scared. I knew she would never do the same for me, and she hasn't. This realization has led me to believe that I am truly the better person—younger, wiser, and more mature. But something told me, something gave me the sense that Charlotte knew this, and she couldn't stand it.

Her overwhelming hatred for me began after we attended Colin Murphy's housewarming party. According to Charlotte, he was a friend from school, but despite attending the same school, I had never seen him. I later heard from a few old friends that Colin had dropped out of East Bridge High a few years ago and had been involved in drug dealing since. He was much older than my sister, so I was unsure how they knew each other. While I knew Charlotte was unpredictable, I doubted she would ever get mixed up in drugs.

We arrived at the party half an hour late, and Charlotte had already had a few drinks. I hadn't realized she had been drinking when she invited me, and the empty bottles in her car were far from reassuring. She may be older than me, but sometimes I think I was given all the brains. As Charlotte strutted up the footpath leading to the house, five guys winked and whistled at her. She paused to hug three girls and smirked at two others as she walked past.

My sister was undeniably difficult, but she was popular. I paused to admire the house, which resembled a miniature mansion. If the rumours about Colin's involvement in drugs weren't true, then he must be exceptionally good at whatever he did. I walked up the path a few steps behind

Charlotte, and the same guys who fancied her paused to stare at me, as did the girls.

"Hey," one of the guys said, "Haven't seen you around here before."

I smiled and kept walking. He obviously didn't think I looked too young to be there, so I wasn't about to tell him. I passed the girls and smiled as I walked through the door. Inside, I saw my sister hanging off three guys and talking to a fourth who seemed to be leaning quite close to her. She hadn't been there five minutes and already had some major male attention, but come to think of it, so did I. The guys that crowded Charlotte became quite interested in me as I walked into the open room, and this was something my sister did not like. The four guys walked toward me, all producing smiles as they crowded around me.

"Hey," one of them said. He was attractive but not the type of guy I would usually go for.

"Hi," I replied, deciding to make small talk as the situation grew awkward with most of the room's attention now on me.

"I'm Andrew," said the guy standing before me.

"I'm Anna," I responded, shaking his hand.

"And I'm Tony," said another, also taking my hand.

"And this is Jason, and I'm Dave," added another, pointing to himself and his friend.

"So, where are you from? Why haven't we seen you around here before?" Tony asked.

"I live in Bridge… and I don't go out much."

"She doesn't go out at all," Charlotte interjected.

"Who are you here with?" Andrew inquired.

"I came with Charlotte."

"Charlotte Finch?"

"Yes, I'm Anna… Finch," I managed, though I wasn't quite sure why it was so hard to say my last name. I suppose the thought of admitting I was related to Charlotte had slipped my mind, perhaps deliberately.

"Oh, you're the baby birdy," said Dave.

"Cheep, cheep," Jason added, laughing into his drink.

"So, Anna, do you put out?" Andrew asked bluntly.

"Pfft, she doesn't even know what that means," Charlotte interrupted again.

A few girls laughed at my sister's remark, but there were others who glared at her and turned back to me with sympathetic expressions. Charlotte was both popular and despised.

"Sure, she does," said a voice from behind the group of guys who had crowded closer to me.

"Hey Colin," Charlotte called out, raising her voice to gain his attention, but Colin kept walking…toward me.

"I bet you're lots of fun, Anna," he said, pushing through the group of guys to stand right in front of me. "You're a pretty little Finch."

"I said, Hey Colin," Charlotte repeated, raising her voice.

"I know, I heard you," he growled back, turning his attention to me again. "So, what are you doing here, Anna?"

"I brought her here," Charlotte interjected. "Clearly that was a mistake. Thought the little dweeb might have some fun…"

"Shut it, Charlotte," Colin snapped. "I was talking to Anna. Now bugger off and make yourself useful."

Charlotte scoffed at the vulgar suggestion, storming out of the room with two girls following close behind.

"So, Anna Finch, do you put out?" Tony asked.

I felt bad for Charlotte and had had enough of this 'chit chat,' so I left the group of guys and followed my sister. As I turned a corner, I overheard a conversation, and the voice sounded a lot like Charlotte.

"Flipping moron doesn't get out much, now I know she's nothing but a whore. I try to do something nice," she sobbed, "But it gets thrown in my face."

I truly felt bad for my sister, but I didn't understand why she was speaking about me like that. I hadn't done anything wrong. Those guys approached me; I was merely being polite and friendly.

"Hey Charlotte, I'm really sorry…"

"Piss off, Anna. You humiliated me."

"I'm sorry, they mean nothing to me; it was nothing."

"Oh, bullshit. I shouldn't have brought you here. I should have left you at home to be the little nerd that you are."

"Charlotte…"

"I said piss off, you little creep. Find your own way home."

Tears swelled in my eyes and a lump formed in my throat. Charlotte was always difficult, but she had never spoken to me like that before. I turned and walked straight out, barging my way through the group of guys that now hovered too close to the doorway. The fresh air was cool on my face as warm tears wetted my cheeks.

"Where are you going, sweetheart?" Tony called after me, but I kept walking.

In ten minutes, I had managed to walk seven blocks and through two parks, moving briskly as I felt I was being followed since leaving the party. The night air was cold and sharp; goosebumps prickled my skin, and the hair on the back of my neck stood on end, urging me to run. I was still ten blocks from home, and there were no cars in sight. The houses I passed were dark, their occupants either out or fast asleep.

The night was eerily quiet, too quiet for my liking. I found myself in an unfamiliar park, which I guessed was Jenson Park, the only park around for kilometres with such a dense canopy of trees. It was dark. Too dark. Something told me I should have stayed on the well-lit street. The moon had vanished behind the treetops, and the leaves began to shake violently as a breeze swept through the dark wood. I slowed down to catch my breath, making the ill-advised decision to turn in circles until I lost my footing and fell to the hard ground.

I sat up, disoriented, unsure of which direction I was headed. Every tree looked the same, and I realized I was lost. Alone. In a dark, forest-like park, with no one knowing where I was. I cursed myself for ever leaving home, for going to the party with Charlotte. And then it hit me. Charlotte.

I reached into my pocket and pulled out my mobile, dialling Charlotte. I listened as the phone rang out. I redialled and waited again, but she did not answer. On the third attempt, she finally picked up.

"What?" snapped Charlotte.

"Charlotte, I'm lost. Can you please come pick me up?"

"Why should I? I told you to find your own way home," she snapped again.

"Charlotte, I know you're angry and you have every right to hate me, but please, I need your help."

"Where are you?"

"I think I'm in Jenson Park. I'm lost in the trees. It's dark and cold."

"Okay," she sighed.

"Are you coming?" I pushed.

"Just stay there," she snapped again, and then she was gone.

Just as I was about to put my phone back in my pocket, I pressed on the Map App and searched for my location. I thought that maybe I could find my way home or at least to the street, and then Charlotte would be able to spot me. But every time I tried to refresh the app; a notice flashed on the screen reading 'Location Unknown.' Maybe I wasn't in Jenson Park. I dialled Charlotte's number again, but it went straight to voicemail. I slid my phone into my pocket and sat against a tree while I waited for my sister.

Two hours passed as I waited for Charlotte, checking my phone every five minutes in case I missed a call or received a message. I wanted to call Dad at his office, but I was afraid of the consequences I would face once he found out I went to a party with Charlotte. Though I thought about telling him that I wasn't interested in drinking and that I planned to be home by 11 PM to finish my assignment, which was the absolute truth. As I thought about it, I realized I'd rather face some moronic punishment from my father than catch pneumonia. I dialled my father's number and waited, but it rang out. I reached his voicemail and decided to leave a message.

"Hey Dad, it's Anna. I'm lost and I need you to come get me. I called Charlotte two hours ago, but she still hasn't arrived. I believe I'm in J..."

The message abruptly ended as my phone emitted a final beep. I glanced at the screen, now lifeless and dark. Attempts to revive it were futile; the battery had completely drained. Frustrated, I shoved the phone back into my pocket and sighed in exasperation, fervently wishing Charlotte would appear in her car to rescue me. Without the phone's light to signal my location, I felt utterly stranded in the dark woods.

As I sat there, tears welled up in my eyes once more that night. I regretted leaving the house, cursed my sister's unreliability, and lamented my father's perpetual absence. Yet, I knew that crying was a fruitless endeavour.

I sat still and silent until I could no longer feel below my waist, sensing that something was amiss. Raising my head from my folded arms, my heart nearly stopped. The moonlight filtered through the treetops, briefly illuminating my surroundings. In that fleeting moment, I wished for the darkness to return. Just a few metres ahead, a tall, dark figure loomed, growing larger as it approached.

I attempted to scramble to my feet, but my legs were numb. As I struggled, crouching on the ground, a hard, blunt object—likely a boot—struck my stomach. I collapsed, clutching my abdomen, only to be struck again, this time in the ribs. Gasping for breath, I felt cold hands grip the back of my neck, tightening their hold. A knee pressed into my back, forcing me further into the dirt, stomach face down. The stranger grappled at the waist of my pants.

I wanted to scream, needed to scream, but no sound emerged. My breaths came in short, rapid gasps as dizziness overtook me. On the verge of unconsciousness, a single thought consumed me: was I about to die? Numbness spread through my body, and a sickening realization settled in the pit of my stomach—Charlotte wasn't coming. She had never intended to.

I let out a loud cry as tears streamed down my face. My cry was met with a blow to the head. A piercing ring filled my ears, and I suddenly saw white. I closed my eyes and let my mind drift. I found myself in a beautiful, endless field of wildflowers. The air was filled with the sweet scent of blossoms and the gentle hum of bees. I was wearing a soft pink linen robe with long sleeves that fluttered in the breeze.

As I lay in the field, I listened to the melodious songs of birds, their tunes weaving through the air like a delicate symphony. The breeze tickled my nose, and I felt the sun's warm kiss on my skin, wrapping me in a comforting embrace.

A monarch butterfly fluttered gracefully through the air, its vibrant wings catching the sunlight. It landed gently on my hand, its delicate legs barely brushing my skin. I watched in awe, feeling a sense of peace and connection with the world around me. But then, reality tugged at the edges of my consciousness. I knew this was just a dream, a fleeting escape from the harshness of my truth. Yet, for a moment, it felt so real, so tangible. I held onto that feeling, savouring the tranquillity it brought.

2

"What were you thinking, leaving her out there alone?" my father's voice boomed.

"I was going to go get her..." came the faint, almost inaudible voice of my sister. Though I was unconscious, I could somehow hear them.

"After two hours? Don't feed me your nonsense, Charlotte; you had no intention of finding your sister. Do you even care? Do you feel any guilt or empathy for Anna? What if she had died?"

My father was yelling, and for once, I thought Charlotte might be crying, that she might feel remorse. But those thoughts vanished as quickly as they came.

"She humiliated me in front of my friends, Dad."

A long silence followed before my father spoke again, his voice now dangerously calm.

"How dare you," he whispered, almost too softly to hear. "How dare you make this about yourself when your sister is lying in that hospital bed, fighting for her life. You care more about yourself than anyone else in this family, Charlotte. Show some compassion, for Christ's sake."

My father paused again, reacting to something Charlotte had said, though this time she spoke too softly for anyone else to hear.

"She deserved it!"

It was a breath of a whisper, cold as ice and death itself. The next sound was a loud snap that echoed through the room—the sound of a slap, flesh against flesh, hand against cheek. I knew Charlotte had just been brought into line.

"Nobody in their right mind—no, in their entire life— deserves what happened to your sister. It pains me to say this, but I am so glad your mother is not here to see how much of a disappointment you've become. Now get out of my sight before I tell you to leave and never come back."

There was a long silence after that, and I wished I could open my eyes. I could hear everything as if I were awake, but no matter how hard I tried, my eyes remained shut. I attempted to move my fingers and toes, but it felt as though my brain was disconnected from my body. Despite this, I felt a faint pressure on my left hand, followed by the sound of a stool scraping against the floor. I realized my father had sat down next to the bed and taken my hand in his, gently squeezing it as he spoke.

"I'm so sorry, Anna," he sobbed. "I'm so sorry I couldn't be there."

The next voice I heard was unfamiliar—deep, rough, but calm. A man's voice. The stool screeched against the floor again as my father stood, his hand slipping away from mine.

"Mr. Finch, I am Senior Constable Stevens, and I am handling Anna's…"

"She hasn't even woken up yet," my father interrupted.

"Yes, we are aware of this, Mr. Finch, but in the meantime, I would like to ask you a few questions regarding the incident," said Senior Constable Stevens.

"Yeah, fine then."

"Mr. Finch, do you know what Anna was doing in the middle of Jenson Park around the time she called you?"

"No, I don't. She called me, but I was working late that night and didn't even hear my phone ring. She left a message saying she was lost and needed me to come find her. She mentioned that Charlotte was supposed to pick her up, but she had already been waiting two hours for her."

"Mr. Finch…"

"Please, call me Mark."

"…Would you happen to know why Charlotte failed to pick up Anna when she explicitly stated she would?"

"Explicitly stated…?"

"We have reason to believe that Anna remained in Jenson Park, waiting for her sister. This is based on the message retrieved from your voicemail."

"She was lost, that's why she stayed," my father responded, panic evident in his voice as he tried to defend Charlotte. "Charlotte is an irresponsible teen, but this is hardly her fault."

"Mr. Finch, we are not suggesting that Charlotte is to blame. We simply need to gather some information."

"I understand."

"We have already spoken to Charlotte. She informed us that she took Anna to a party, but things became heated between them after a conversation. Charlotte mentioned that she saw Anna leave with someone and assumed this person would take her home. Now, Mr. Finch, how would you describe the relationship between your daughters?"

"It's okay, I guess. They're not the best of friends, but they're civil. It's been hard since my wife died."

"We understand and are sorry for your loss, Mr. Finch."

"You keep saying 'we'."

"Yes, the department and myself…"

Their conversation was interrupted by a nurse, who asked both Senior Constable Stevens and my father to leave, as the other patients in the room needed rest.

"Before I leave, Mr. Finch, I need you to describe what happened when you found your daughter in Jenson Park in the early hours of that morning."

19

There was a long silence, and I wasn't sure if they had left or if my father was even going to provide the information. But in a very low voice, my father began to speak.

"It was 2 a.m. when I checked my messages before heading home. As soon as I heard Anna's voice, I got into my car and drove home to see if she was there. When she wasn't, I got Charlotte out of bed and asked if she knew where her sister was. After some arguing, Charlotte frowned when she saw that Anna was not asleep in her own bed, where she expected her to be. Charlotte didn't cry or look worried at all when she told me she had taken Anna to a party. She said they had had a fight, and that Anna had humiliated her in front of her friends. I asked Charlotte what she meant, but she didn't answer. I then asked if Anna had called her. She was reluctant to tell me the truth until finally, she admitted that Anna had said she was lost in Jenson Park and needed her to come and find her."

"Of course, I was furious with Charlotte but punishing her wasn't something I was about to do without finding my other daughter first. I drove to Jenson Park with Charlotte in the passenger seat, having to drag her there. She didn't seem interested in her sister's whereabouts, which struck me as odd. Even when I found Anna, Charlotte didn't seem to care."

"How did you find your daughter, Mr. Finch?"

"She was face down in the dirt," he choked, "Her clothes torn and bloodied. Her skin was pale and ice cold… she was covered in black bruises."

"On what area of Anna's body would you say the majority of the bruises were?" asked Senior Constable Stevens.

"Her thighs and lower back," my father whispered, sniffling, "She was bleeding."

"What did you do when you found your daughter?"

"I turned her over and checked her pulse to make sure she was still alive. She had scratches all over her from the sticks and rocks; dirt covered her face and hair. There was bruising around her throat. Charlotte just stood there, expressionless. I wrapped my coat around Anna to warm and comfort her. For a split second, she opened her eyes and looked at me. Her eyes moved to Charlotte, and then she was unconscious again. I took her into my arms, walked to the car, and drove her to the hospital."

That was the last thing I heard before I drifted into a deeper sleep, remaining that way for several days. When I finally woke, I was alone. I tried to sit up in the hospital bed, but my body screamed in pain. I uncovered my legs to find them black and bruised, covered in cuts. Large yellow and purple bruises circled both my thighs. I winced as I sat up, feeling pain in my stomach. There was a dull ache in my groin and lower back, compelling me to lie down again.

"Oh, no. You mustn't sit up," said a nurse as she walked in.

I watched her check my chart and the machines that were hooked up to me.

"Why am I here?" I asked, my throat dry and coarse. I suddenly found myself extremely thirsty. The nurse must have read my mind as she poured me a cup of icy cold water.

"You were hurt, love. I'll call your father and let him know you're awake."

The nurse disappeared. I drank three cups of water and crunched on some ice as I waited. I frowned as the brief conversation replayed in my mind. I remembered what happened; I was there. I could still feel his hands around my throat and his knee in my back as he pushed me toward the ground. My heart started racing, and a lump formed in my throat as I relived it again. But just like before, nobody came to my rescue.

I started to panic, and the machines next to me began making all kinds of loud beeping noises. I clutched my ears, tears flowing from my eyes. I didn't want to be here. I wanted to be in my own bed, in my own house. I wanted Douglas. I wanted my mother.

"Calm down, Anna," said a nurse as she walked in. "Everything is okay now, love. You're safe."

"Where's my dad?" I sobbed. "I want my father."

"He's on his way; he will be here soon."

"Is she allowed other visitors?" said a voice.

My heart slowed, and my blood rushed as my eyes met his. His brown eyes stared into mine, his mouth curled into a slight smile, his lips as pink and plump and perfect as always. I looked him up and down as the tears ceased, and I wiped my nose. He was masculine and tan. His brown hair was short but as curly as ever. He held a bunch of flowers in one hand and a small brown teddy bear in the other. The nurse watched me for a moment and decided it was okay now that I wasn't in such a panic. She left us alone and closed the curtain behind her.

"Richard."

"Hey Anna, I brought you these."

He handed me the flowers and the teddy bear, his eyes filled with sympathy. I stared back, my heart fluttering slightly. I metaphorically kicked myself for ever letting Charlotte come between us. He was perfect in every way, and I found myself missing him dearly as he leaned in to hug me. His cologne was intoxicating.

"How are you?"

"I'm okay," I replied, though we both knew I wasn't.

A long silence stretched between us. Richard looked at me as if he had so much to say but didn't know where to start.

"Has Charlotte been to see you?" he asked.

"No, you're the first person. I just woke up."

"You seem pretty calm for someone who just woke up from a coma."

"A coma? How long was I asleep?"

"Three weeks," he answered, frowning.

"Does everyone at school know?"

Richard nodded slowly; his expression sympathetic.

"Charlotte is kind of boasting about it."

"Boasting? What is she saying?"

"One minute she's saying you deserved it, and the next she's acting all depressed. Just attention-seeking stuff. She won't shut up."

"But she doesn't care?"

I didn't know why I asked that. I knew Charlotte didn't care about me; she only cared for herself.

"It doesn't look that way. A lot of people feel sorry for you and think Charlotte is cruel."

"I don't know why they feel sorry for me. People get mugged every day."

"Anna, you weren't mugged," he frowned again.

I glared at him in exasperation, not understanding my sudden anger.

"What do you mean?"

He paused, hesitating, but then changed his mind and sat silently. Tears welled in his eyes as he looked down.

"That guy really hurt you, Anna. He almost killed you."

"But he didn't, and I'm fine."

"You're not fine. Look at you," he snapped, pain evident in his eyes. "You're all beaten up... and I can't imagine what else."

"The police will find him..."

"They did, Anna. They found him dead in his own apartment. He killed himself."

"What?"

"They found him last week. He must have known they were onto him. He can't do time because he's dead."

Hearing that was a shock to my system; it was a lot to take in having just woken from a coma. I wondered if my dad would have given me the same information.

"Do you think I'll still be questioned?"

"I don't know. Hopefully not, they can't use it anyway."

"So... were you at the party?"

"No, I wasn't invited, but I had heard about it. I wouldn't have gone anyway, and luckily, I didn't. The cops showed up around 1:30 p.m., busted Colin Murphy dealing.

Apparently, the police have been after him for months; they just needed to catch him in the act."

"Wow. That's huge."

"Yeah, but not as huge as what happened to you."

"Oh, please. There's no need for a comparison."

He frowned at me again, as if I weren't taking the situation seriously enough.

"But still, I'm glad you're alive."

"Richard," interrupted my father as he walked into the room, "Nice to see you, it's been a while."

Richard stood to greet my dad with a handshake.

"Mark," greeted Richard, "Yes, too long."

"How are you, sweetheart?" Dad asked, turning to face me.

It was the first time in a long while that I had heard him call me sweetheart. Given my current situation, I understood, but it still sounded odd.

"I'm sore, tired, and a little confused."

"What are you confused about, darling?"

There it was again. I knew my father meant no harm and that he wanted to comfort me, to be more affectionate and sensitive toward me, but it just didn't feel right. Just because I was in the hospital and in that state, he felt the need to use pet names like that. It wasn't flattering; it felt like a mask, a temporary wall he put up to hide his true alcoholic, don't-give-a-damn-about-anyone-but-myself demeanour. Sometimes I thought it was scary how alike my father and Charlotte could be. But perhaps I was overthinking it. Maybe he was sensitive and afraid because he almost lost me. Maybe it was his way of dealing with the pain, like how he resorted to alcohol to ease the pain of losing Mum when he should have sought comfort in his family.

"Anna? What are you confused about?"

The previous thought eluded my mind as the real reason for my confusion surfaced. Tears threatened as a lump formed in my throat once more.

"Why didn't she come, Dad?" I whispered, my voice breaking. "I was so scared. And cold."

Dad put his arms around me, holding my head close to his chest as he sat on the bed next to me. Richard had already made a silent exit. My whole body shook as I sobbed into my father's t-shirt, drenching it with my tears.

"I don't know, Anna," he said quite sternly. I knew he was still angry with my sister, and it was clear the situation was unresolved.

"She told me she'd be there… and she wasn't."

"I know, sweetie. I will talk to her later on when I get home… if she is home."

I cried for what seemed like forever, until my tears ran dry, and I just didn't have the energy anymore.

"Does she even care, Dad?" I managed through sobs.

"Of course she does."

"Then why isn't she here? Why hasn't she come?"

"I don't know, Anna. I don't know what's going on with her."

3

The next day, I was scheduled to see two people: Senior Constable Stevens for questioning and a psychologist to assess if I was ready to go home. I truly hoped I was. I was dying to see Douglas, my chubby Basset hound.

"Miss Finch, I am Senior Constable Stevens, and this is Constable O'Riley."

The two police officers sat in the chairs to the left of my bed, one a man and the other a woman. Another woman, dressed in white, stood to my right—the psychologist. She held a notepad and pen, her eyes twitchy as she prepared to take notes.

"We are here today to take a statement from you. Are you aware that the perpetrator is deceased?"

"Yes."

"Do you understand that due to these circumstances, anything you tell us cannot be used against him as he is no longer able to serve punishment for his crimes committed against you?"

"Yes, but if he is dead… why do you need a statement from me?"

The female officer, O'Riley, looked at me with a soft expression as she spoke.

"Anna, we need to know exactly what happened so that we may report it and then determine the next steps, though there isn't much we can do anymore. We know who did this to you, and we are very sorry that he cannot be sentenced, but at least he is dead and cannot harm anyone else."

"Think of it as a closing statement," added Senior Constable Stevens. "Once we take this statement from you, you can go back to your normal life and hopefully overcome this whole ordeal."

I knew he meant well, and he was a respectable man, but I couldn't bring myself to look at him. He was a stranger to me. From that moment, I knew it would be hard to ever trust men again—not men like Dad or Richard, but men I didn't know and hadn't met before.

"Will you be okay if we ask you a few questions?" asked O'Riley.

"Yes."

"Okay. Ms Finch, did you attend Colin Murphy's party with your older sister Charlotte on the night of May 11th this year?"

"Yes."

"Did you want to go? Did your sister insist that you accompany her in any way?"

"Well, I was doing a school assignment when she came to my room saying she was invited to a party. She didn't say who. She then asked if I wanted to go with her. At first, I didn't want to, but then I decided to go for just a few hours. I wanted to be home by 11 p.m. so I could finish my schoolwork. I know I am underage and didn't plan on drinking..."

"It's okay, Anna. Do you feel that Charlotte persuaded your decision in any way? Did she say anything to you that changed your mind?"

"Well, yes... she called me a party pooper and then said Richard was going to be there."

"Who is Richard?"

"My ex-boyfriend."

"I see," said Constable O'Riley. "Was Richard at the party?"

"No, he told me yesterday that he wasn't invited and wouldn't have gone anyway."

"What happened at the party to make you want to leave? Did someone make you feel uncomfortable? Did anyone say anything to you that you found strange?"

"Well, there were a group of boys that surrounded me for a little while. They asked me questions..."

"What kind of questions, Anna?"

"One of them asked if I put out. Charlotte overheard the conversation and told everyone that I didn't even know what that meant."

"Did Charlotte interrupt the conversation at any other time?"

"Yes, Colin Murphy came up to me and said hello. I don't think Charlotte liked that very much because she tried to get his attention, but when he kept talking to me, she got frustrated and walked out."

"After Charlotte left the room, did you see her again that night?"

"Yes, I followed her, but she told me to leave."

A lump formed in my throat as I thought of the things Charlotte had said to me. Tears threatened my eyes.

"How did she tell you to leave?"

"She told me to piss off and find my own way home…"

"Had Charlotte ever spoken to you like that before?"

"No, she was always nasty, but she never said those words to me before. She was meaner than usual."

"Anna, I know you want to protect your sister, but did it seem as though she had taken something that night? Did she seem different?"

"You mean drugs? No, I don't think Charlotte is that stupid. She drinks quite heavily… and drives, but I don't think she would ever touch anything like that."

"Was Charlotte drinking heavily at the party?"

"She had been drinking before we left home."

I froze as the words slipped from my mouth. I had just dobbed on my sister for driving under the influence.

"It's okay, Anna. It's important that you tell us the truth."

"Will Charlotte get into trouble because I told you that?"

"Unfortunately, we can't make an arrest based purely on an accusation; in this case, what you've told us. We could question her, but it's not likely she will tell us the truth."

"Are you worried about telling us things that could get your sister into trouble?" asked Constable O'Riley.

"Yes."

"That's understandable, but we are here today to discuss what happened to you on May 11th of this year. At the moment, we are just trying to make sense of what happened leading up to the assault."

"I went to the party with my sister. We had an argument. She told me to find my own way home, so I did. I walked out and was walking home in the dark, alone. But I found myself lost in Jenson Park. I called Charlotte for help; she said she would come, so I waited. I waited around for two hours in the cold. I felt as though I was being followed and then… found out I had been. The moon came out, and I could see…"

"It's alright, Anna," said Constable O'Riley in a soft voice. "You don't have to say anymore."

"Is there anything else you need to tell us, Anna?" asked Senior Constable Stevens.

"No, I've told you everything."

"Anna, could you please read this statement to yourself and, if it is all correct, please sign the bottom once you've finished."

Senior Constable Stevens handed me the handwritten statement he had scrawled down as I recounted what had happened. I read over it and signed the bottom with my name. They had managed to write down everything, yet I didn't see the point in doing so; the man who attacked me had killed himself. He more or less got away with it. He attacked me, and I'll forever be scarred for life, but I can't help but feel sad for him. He either took the easy way out of prison time or genuinely felt a sense of guilt and regret for what he did to me.

"Before we go, is there anything else you wish to ask?"

"I would like to know the name of my attacker…"

"And why is this, Miss Finch?"

"Closure."

It was the only thing of which I could think. He was dead, but I wanted to know his name, even though I didn't know why. It felt like a sense of closure, even if it didn't make sense.

"David Hagan," said Constable O'Riley, and walked out with a gentle smile.

David Hagan. I knew his name. But it was just a name now, nothing more. I sat in silence for a few moments, my mind blank. I stared into space until the psychologist decided to introduce herself.

"Hi Anna, I'm Lucia. Is it okay if we have a chat?"

"Sure."

"How are you feeling?"

"Physically or emotionally?"

"Well, both I suppose. Let's start with physically?"

"I'm sore, stiff, and tired."

"And what about emotionally?"

"I've never been more confused, sad, and angry in all my life."

"What are you confused about?"

"A number of things."

"Well, let's start with the first."

"Why David Hagan chose to attack me."

I said it like I knew the man. It sounded as though I knew him. But I didn't.

"I know I can't answer all your questions correctly, Anna. But maybe I could shed a little light on the situation.

Help you think about them and possibly answer them for yourself. From what I see, I know you're a very bright girl. You have feelings, which make you an understanding and tolerant person. Could you think of any reasons why David Hagan attacked you and then committed suicide?"

"I don't know the man. How could I find reasons for why a stranger did what he did?"

"Well, let me tell you this. David Hagan was a lonely man. A man with many problems; he was misunderstood, slow, and unemployed, surviving on a pension. He couldn't read or write well and had a daughter he could never love."

"He had a daughter. Why couldn't he love her?"

"The mother of his child took her away. She didn't want her to see who her father was. She kept her daughter away from him because she saw him as an embarrassment."

"That's awful. But how do you know this?"

"Anna, I'm a psychologist, a psychologist... a doctor. I have records and an understanding of people that you could not fathom. I read people—their emotions, the way they walk, talk, eat, or answer questions. The way they ask questions and how they listen. But mostly, I read their eyes. It is a gift."

"Did you know David Hagan?"

"Yes."

The room was silent for what seemed like an hour. I didn't know what to say. I had so many questions but didn't know where to start.

"Are you okay, Anna?"

"I don't know. I mean, how did you know him?"

"He came to me years ago. He felt he needed help. He needed someone to talk to…"

"Aren't you breaking some type of confidentiality by telling me this?"

"He's dead, Anna. The contract is void."

I suddenly found myself lost for words. This therapist seemed inappropriate and outspoken.

"So, he was…once…innocent?"

"Very much so."

"And because you knew him before this… you feel sorry for him?"

"No. He will forever be guilty for what he did to you, dead or alive. But I believe that he only attacked you in a time of weakness."

"So, you want me to forgive him?"

I was suddenly angry.

"No, Anna…"

"Then why are you here? What do you want?"

"I want you to understand the minds of people around you."

"You want to give me a lesson on psychoanalysis? Why?"

"Anna, I just want you to understand why people do things. Why David Hagan attacked you. Why Charlotte is afraid of loving you."

"This isn't about my sister. Did you come here to talk to me about Charlotte?"

"Yes."

"Because you think you know Charlotte?"

"Well…"

"Because you don't."

But I did. I knew exactly how Charlotte's mind worked. I knew deep down that she didn't feel guilty for leaving me there in the cold and dark. Not once has she ever taken any responsibility for her actions, including now.

"You have every right to be angry, Anna. But try to understand why you are angry?"

"I'm angry because my sister left me cold, scared, and alone in the middle of a forest. I'm angry because Charlotte is a self-centred person; she only cares about herself. I'm angry because she hates me, and I don't know why…"

"Have you ever thought that she might be jealous, Anna?"

"Jealous of what? She has nothing to be jealous about."

"She has in her mind. Anna, we don't exactly know what goes on inside Charlotte's head, but we do know that she's human and has a heart. She might act as though she doesn't care about you, but deep down, she does. She hasn't come to visit, has she?"

"No."

"And do you know why?"

"She doesn't care. She thinks she's done nothing wrong."

"She's put up a wall, Anna. She knows she's done wrong and is devastated by the fact that she almost lost her little sister because of her own stupidity. She feels guilt and regret, but she won't admit it to herself. She's hurt and embarrassed. Because she loves you, Anna."

"Bullshit. Charlotte has no feelings," I snapped, and then it all came out. "Charlotte is the devil. I opened my eyes when my father found me and wrapped me in his jacket. I saw the shock and hurt in his eyes. I looked at Charlotte and saw nothing. Her eyes were empty and black, just like her soul. She looked as if she wished I had died, as if she were disappointed that I lived. And she won't visit because she hates the fact that I'm still alive. She hates that dad loves me. She hated that I was more popular than her, which is why she always screws things up for me with her lies. She couldn't stand seeing me happy, and whatever made me happy, she took away. She's always wanted to be the centre of attention and won't have it any other way. That's another reason she's not here; she can't stand the fact that I'm the centre of attention right now, and I don't want to be. I want a normal life with a normal sister who isn't angry because I'm still alive. I want a sister who doesn't wish I were dead."

I was so angry I was convulsing. Everything that had been on my mind about Charlotte had finally been let out. The glass bottle that held my thoughts and feelings had finally shattered into a million pieces. I looked at Lucia as I caught my breath, but she was lost for words. My throat was sore, and as I looked around the room, a few nurses in the hallway had paused to stare in shock. I hadn't realized that I had been yelling. I was suddenly embarrassed.

"I had no idea your feelings toward Charlotte were like that... and so strong," Lucia said softly, her eyelids fluttering.

"People have bullies; I have a sister..." I whispered, still mortified that I had caused a scene.

"Well, I think that will be enough for today. You need rest."

"Can I go home?"

"Yes, I think you need to be around family. I also think you need to reiterate what family means. I don't want any more of these sudden outbursts the next time I see you. I wish our next meeting to be civil. Good day, Ms Finch."

I couldn't believe it. I stared in shock as she walked out of the room. She thinks I'm wrong about Charlotte. She probably thinks my outburst was a verbal attack against my sister. It was then that I realized I didn't like this woman. I wanted a different psychologist.

I got home that afternoon, frantically greeted by Douglas, who couldn't have been happier to see me. When I opened my bedroom door, it was as if nothing had changed. I had left it in the state it was when I went to the party, apart from my closet doors being open from when Dad got me some clean clothes while I was in the hospital. I packed away my assignments and lay on my bed. Douglas jumped up next to me, licked my arm once, and curled up in a ball beside me. He sighed as if happy I was home. I felt myself slowly drift off to sleep, but it wasn't long until Dad woke me for dinner. It was strange; Dad hadn't sat with us at dinner for a long time. It was a rare occasion.

As we sat quietly at the dinner table, Douglas insisted on sitting right at my feet. It made me smile, as if he were keeping an eye on me to make sure I wouldn't leave again. It was a comfort to know he cared for me so much.

"Did you notice that your sister is home?" Dad asked Charlotte.

I watched for a moment as she rolled her eyes in response, vigorously stabbing her beans with her fork. She sighed in frustration.

"Leave. Now!" snapped Dad.

Charlotte looked at him in shock.

"Are you serious?" she snapped back.

"Yes."

"What the hell for?"

"For your stupid, childish behaviour, Charlotte. I won't have it. She's your sister, and we are a family whether you like it or not."

"I don't. I hate it."

"Well, that's your problem."

Charlotte rose from the table with her plate in hand. She turned to walk away, but Dad grabbed her arm.

"Leave that here."

"Why?"

"Because you're not eating in your room."

"What the hell, Dad? You just told me to leave."

"Yes, due to your childish behaviour. You can come back and finish your dinner when you've realized that we are your family and Anna's not a piece of shit."

Charlotte looked at me with eyes as cold as ice, a small sound escaping her lips.

"Pfft."

"Go to your room, Charlotte," Dad was now shouting.

My sister turned and walked away, mumbling under her breath. It was from that day that Charlotte decided I wasn't good enough to be her sister anymore, or maybe I was too perfect. Whatever it was, she wasn't happy; she went out of her way to make my life miserable. And she did—she made my life a living hell.

4

The next week, I decided to go to school, which seemed like a good idea at the time. But once I walked into the corridor, I suddenly felt the urge to run home. Every single student and teacher paused to stare at me. As I walked to my locker, the crowd started to thin as everyone slowly returned to what they were doing.

"Hey Anna," said Corey McGuire from my English class.

I replied with a smile and kept walking.

"Hi Anna," said Mary Owen, who was leaning against one of the lockers near mine.

She was in my science class. She was nice and spoke to me every now and then, but we weren't that close. Come to think of it, I wasn't really close to anyone anymore since Charlotte ruined every friendship I had ever built. Clara Swivel was my best friend once upon a time, but my sister ruined that too.

"Hi," I said to Mary as I reached my locker.

I fumbled with the keys as I opened my locker. The awkward crowd of students and teachers made me nervous, and even though most of them had already gone to class, I didn't want to turn around to face any of them. But my thoughts got the better of me, and I found myself looking over both my shoulders. At one end of the corridor, I saw Charlotte standing with a group of her so-called friends. She was glaring at me with her ice-cold eyes. It was a deathly stare. I turned to my locker as something slipped out and fell to my feet.

I picked up a single folded sheet of paper. It was a letter. I opened it and scanned over the writing, but there was no name signed at the bottom. Then I frowned to myself. This letter had been typed and printed; the person who wrote it wanted to remain anonymous. I looked over my shoulder again, but everyone had gone to class. There were only five people left in the corridor, including myself. I looked down at the letter in my hands and started reading.

I can't say who I am in case Charlotte finds out, but she's said some really horrible   things   about   you   to other people. She's laughing at what happened to you; she   laughed so hard she had tears in her eyes, and she even clutched her stomach. Your   sister is a horrible person, and I feel so sorry for you, Anna. You're nothing but nice and caring to everyone, and you didn't deserve what happened to you, even though   Charlotte is telling everyone you did. A lot of people are here for you, Anna. We   care!!   Hope you're okay xx

I should have been more surprised, but that was typical Charlotte. She really was a horrible person. I carried the letter for the rest of the day, occasionally reading over it in class. I guessed that the teachers had heard what happened, as they didn't bother me during class. They didn't even ask about the letter in my hand, though Ms Connelly did ask if I was okay as tears threatened my eyes. She seemed concerned and put a hand on my shoulder for a few seconds as she wandered around the room. I suppose nobody else asked me about it because it would have been an awkward conversation. But I was glad; I didn't want to talk about it. I wanted to push it from my mind as if it never happened.

As I sat alone for lunch, a few people stared at me, glaring over their shoulders. Others looked at me with expressions of sympathy. But I didn't want sympathy; I wanted everything to be normal. Clara and two other old friends sat at my table with worried expressions.

"Hey Anna," said Kim. "You looked lonely, so I hope it's okay if we sit with you."

"It's fine," I replied with a smile.

I could feel Clara's eyes on me the whole time. I looked at her briefly, and the expression on her face was lost.

Her eyes told me she was sorry. When Clara and I were best friends, we were inseparable. We knew everything there was to know about each other, and that would never change. I was surprised that after several months, we could still communicate with just an expression. She felt angry with herself for believing Charlotte's lies, but another part of her was different, like she had moved on. She wanted to be friends again, but it would never be the same.

Lucy, the fourth girl at the table, glanced at the letter in my hand and frowned. She then looked at me with sad eyes, but only for a moment before turning to start a conversation with Kim. I sat and glanced at my phone as I signed into Facebook. I skimmed over my newsfeed, pretending to be interested in the things my 'friends' had posted.

I listened to the conversation between Kim and Lucy; they were talking about Jack Norman, a boy from last year's year 12 class. Apparently, he had knocked up a girl from West Bridge and now planned to marry her. I felt Clara's eyes on me for a while, but then something on Facebook caught my attention.

Someone had made a new 'like' page, and five of my Facebook friends had liked it. The page caught my attention because there were two words in its title that startled me: my name. A lump formed in my throat as I read the title of the page, "Go to Hell Anna Finch." I clicked on the page and found that it had been made a week ago and already had 5,000 likes. The page had no photos or information, but I expected that it wouldn't be long until it did. I searched through the likes and found the five Facebook friends of mine who obviously supported the page and found it funny. I read the names: Michael Power, Dex Gunther, Abigail McGowan, Lauren Pennington, and Alyssa Almund. All these people went to my school. I looked around and spotted the four girls sitting together at a table to the right of Charlotte's. They all laughed and chatted until Ruth looked toward me. I saw her elbow Alyssa and Lauren, who both looked toward me as well. Abigail followed their gaze and glared. They all stared at me with spiteful grins, laughing and chatting to each other. It wasn't half obvious that they were talking about me.

"Ignore them, Anna," said Clara, stealing my gaze.

I looked at my Facebook again and unfriended Michael, Dex, Abigail, Lauren, and Alyssa. I also went back into "Go to Hell Anna Finch" and reported the page. I then looked at Clara.

"Hey, there is this page on Facebook called 'Go to Hell Anna Finch.' Could you report it, please?"

It was a whisper, but Clara heard every word I said. She looked shocked that I even spoke to her. We sat in silence for a few moments before she replied.

"I already have. I've reported it five times already."

I was lost for words. I thought this girl, my former best friend, hated me.

"Thanks," I smiled.

She smiled back. Maybe she was starting to see through Charlotte and her web of lies. The bell rang, but I had had enough of school and the students of East Bridge High, so I walked home.

The following days at school were relatively uneventful; the initial buzz surrounding the 'Anna Finch was attacked' story began to fade. People seemed to lose interest, and my ordeal quickly became one of those fleeting 'remember when' anecdotes that are briefly mentioned before moving on to more engaging topics. I was relieved by this shift; I despised being the centre of attention and preferred to blend into the background. However, blending in was something Charlotte could never achieve. She was a show pony, and everyone knew it.

Charlotte liked to believe she had control over the football team, thinking she held sway over each member. Yet, some players ignored her, which drove her to frustration. Richard once confided in me that Charlotte had been involved with most of the football team, sparing only a few who had girlfriends, though even that didn't deter her. The only boys who remained untouched by Charlotte's influence were Richard, Luke, Gary, Sebastian, and Thomas. They were the ones who didn't succumb to her charms or respond to her every beck and call. Those who did were mere puppets, manipulated by Charlotte to do her bidding in exchange for her favours. She would sit in the cafeteria, making out with the football player of the week, often a different boy from year 11 or 12 each week. On one occasion, she was seen kissing two different players within half an hour. It reminded me of all the times she cried over boys, professing her love for them. But Charlotte didn't understand love; she didn't know how to love.

The following Monday, I was eager for a normal school day and hopeful for a great week. However, my optimism quickly dissipated as I entered the school gates. Scattered everywhere were white sheets of paper, and as I picked one up, I saw what everyone else was reading and laughing at. It was another Facebook page, but this time someone had printed it out for all to see. The page was titled "Let's Hate Anna Finch," featuring a picture labelled "Anna 'Sharky' Finch" with my face superimposed on a shark's body. The photograph was painfully familiar; I hated how I looked in it. Unlike Charlotte, who flaunted her perfect teeth and million-dollar smile, I had always been self-conscious about my crooked teeth and rarely smiled in photos. In this picture, I was laughing, exposing my uneven teeth. The only people who knew how self-conscious I was about my teeth were Charlotte and my father. The only person who could have accessed this photo was my sister.

My blood rushed and I was suddenly furious. I started picking up every piece of paper I could get my hands on; three girls from year 7 helped me. I shoved them into the nearest bin and started to walk away. I turned as Thomas Larkmen from my year lit a cigarette behind the building. I stormed toward him and demanded his lighter.

"Geez, are you alright, Anna?" he asked, his expression blank.

I didn't reply. Instead, I marched toward the bin and set its contents on fire. I knew I would probably face a week of detention or even expulsion, but I didn't care. I had no intention of staying at school that day, not when I'd be called "Sharky" and tormented, asked to bare my crooked teeth for everyone's amusement. I handed Thomas back his lighter and stormed off in search of my sister.

When I found her, I was livid. I wanted to slap her hard across the face. In her hands was a thick pile of paper, more of the Facebook printouts I had just burned. Her two friends, Mirandah, and Danielle, stood beside her, each holding their own piles. Furious, I walked right up to my sister. As she turned to face me, I punched her in the nose. Blood gushed from her nostrils and filled her mouth as she gasped in shock and disbelief. Mirandah and Danielle dropped the printouts and walked away, just as shocked as Charlotte.

"Charlotte Finch, you are the devil. How dare you do this to me?" I yelled, my voice echoing with fury. She squinted, clutching her nose in pain. "I have done nothing to you. You are a bully and a whore, and you will get what's coming."

"Oh, what are you going to do, you pathetic loser?" she sneered.

"Nothing. I will let karma do the dirty work for me."

"Pfft! Piss off."

"Do you know what happens to spider's webs, Charlotte?"

But she had no answer; she frowned at me as if I spoke a foreign language.

"They fall apart, Charlotte. And that's exactly what's going to happen to you and your vindictive web of lies. People will soon see your true colours and they will leave, and you will be left with nobody. Not even me."

We stood in the middle of the schoolyard, surrounded by onlookers. I glanced at my sister, but she was speechless. Mirandah and Danielle quickly joined her, armed with a box of tissues and her makeup bag, casting malevolent glares in my direction. Two more people to unfriend on Facebook, I thought, just as a hard object struck the back of my head. My ears rang, and I felt a wave of dizziness. I looked down to see a football bouncing and rolling to a stop. As I turned, another football hit me squarely on the side of the face.

"Stop it!" came a familiar voice.

It was Richard. I looked over to see the football team gathered in a large group. One of the boys from year 12 aimed his football at me, but this time Richard pushed him in the chest.

"I said stop it," he yelled. "You've had your fun. Now piss off before I tell the coach."

The crowd began to thin as people started to leave. Many of the year 7 students lingered, captivated by the unexpected schoolyard drama.

"Are you okay?" Richard asked, gently placing his hand on my face. "That's going to bruise. Come on, I'll take you home to ice it."

I followed him to his car, passing Thomas, Luke, and Sebastian on the way.

"Where are you going, man?" asked Luke.

"Taking Anna home to ice her face."

"You'll be back for practice, yeah?"

"Yeah, tell coach I'll be there."

"Who was it?" asked Thomas.

"Bentley and Miles."

"Ah, we'll get them in practice. Don't worry, Anna."

Thomas winked as he turned to walk away, followed by Luke.

"Take care of your face, Anna," said Sebastian.

I walked into the house, straight into dad. He looked at my face in shock.

"She made a horrible picture… she put my face on a shark's body, using a photo I hate because of my teeth. It's on Facebook."

I took out my phone, opened Facebook, and showed him the image. He frowned, shaking his head in frustration.

"Are you sure that Charlotte did this?"

"Yes, she's the only person who could have. That photo was hidden away in my bedroom, so she went to a lot of trouble to do this to me."

"Is that why you gave her a bleeding nose?"

"Yes! She deserved it."

"Well, the school didn't tell me that she hit you back."

"She didn't."

He raised a hand to my face and brushed my hair away, revealing a faint bruise starting to show on my cheekbone.

"Then who gave you that?"

I was going to tell him, but I knew the football team would do worse if they found out I ratted them out.

"I tripped on my school bag," I lied.

"You must have hit the ground pretty hard."

"It was a face plant, Dad. Of course it was hard."

"Well, make sure you put some ice on that. I have to go back to work. I only came home to get some paperwork."

"Are you still angry at me?"

"No, I'll tell the school what happened. But they expect you to do some detention or community service or replace the bin."

"Yeah, I really didn't think it through."

"I won't be home for dinner tonight, so cook yourself something and eat in your room. It might be best to stay away from your sister."

"Okay."

I watched him get into his car and drive away. I winced as I brushed my hair off my face, forgetting about my bruised cheekbone. I found a bag of frozen peas in the freezer and placed it on my face while I sprawled out on the lounge and turned on the television.

5

The next morning, Douglas woke me with his incessant barking. I climbed out of bed and went into the backyard to see what was troubling him. On the grass beneath the walnut tree lay two featherless baby birds. Douglas barked frantically from a few feet away, unwilling to approach the strange creatures. Their eyes were still closed, and their necks were stretched out as they cheeped for their mother. Looking up, I saw that the bottom of the nest had fallen out, but the mother was nowhere to be seen. I hurried to the garden shed and retrieved a cardboard box. Carefully, I picked up the baby birds and placed them gently in the box, lining it with old straw from the garden to make them comfortable. I took them inside and waited for Douglas with the door open, but he remained outside, sniffing the air before sitting on the grass. Realizing he wasn't coming in; I closed the door.

As I turned to walk through the kitchen, the doorbell rang. I glanced at the clock on the kitchen wall; it was 8:30 a.m., quite early for a visitor. I answered the door and found Lucia standing there. I wasn't exactly thrilled, but I still had many visits scheduled with her.

"Good morning, Anna. How are you feeling today?"

"Fine, I guess."

"You guess? Did something happen at school?"

I glanced at her inquisitively, sensing that she already knew about the previous day's events.

"No," I lied, wanting to gauge how much she knew.

She stared at me in silence for a long time, likely studying me, reading my eyes. I tried to maintain the pretence that there was nothing to tell. How good she was at her job, I didn't know, but I really didn't want to talk about Charlotte.

"Thank you," she finally said.

"For what?"

"For showing me what you look like when you lie to me, Anna."

"I didn't lie," I lied.

"Oh, Anna. Please, stop. I spoke to your teachers and your father yesterday afternoon. I know what happened and I think we should talk about it."

"Charlotte's a bitch, end of story."

"Without the foul language, please."

"Fine," I sighed in defeat.

I honestly didn't like talking to this woman about my sister, whom I considered evil, because she believed that Charlotte meant no harm at all. Our last conversation hadn't been very productive, especially since I had snapped, revealing emotions that had been bottled up for a long time. And, of course, new emotions that had only surfaced in the past few weeks—a sense of hatred and loathing toward Charlotte. But who wouldn't hate a bully? I seriously didn't understand this woman or her methods for solving problems.

"So, tell me what happened. From the beginning," she prompted.

"But you already know," I frowned.

"Yes, but I want you to tell me. But first, let's go inside."

I let the door swing open as Lucia made her way inside. She navigated to the lounge room with ease, which struck me as odd. I frowned again.

"Oh, yes. I have been here before; I came to visit your dad when you were in the hospital. I tried to speak to Charlotte, but she's a tough one."

"What did you and my father talk about?" I asked, still frowning.

"How he was coping with everything, and how he was managing without your mother. But Anna, please, you mustn't frown."

I sat on the lounge opposite her and waited for her to say something else, but she urged me to begin. So, I did. The sooner this conversation was over, the sooner she could leave.

"I arrived at school yesterday morning to find these printouts from a Facebook page someone had made. It was called 'Let's Hate Anna Finch,' or something like that. There was a picture of a shark with my face photoshopped onto its body. The title of the picture was 'Anna Sharky Finch,' I think. The printouts were everywhere. I gathered as many as I could and put them in a bin... and set it on fire. I wanted to destroy as many as I could, but when I found my sister, she had a large stack in her arms, as did her two friends, Mirandah, and Danielle. I was so angry; I couldn't contain myself. I punched Charlotte in the nose and yelled at her."

"What did you say to her?" she asked.

"I told her that her plans would eventually fail, that her web of lies would collapse, and so would she. She asked what I was going to do, but I said I would let karma take care of her."

"What's your understanding of karma, Anna?"

"Do good things, and good things will happen. Do bad things, and bad things will happen."

"So, you believe that all these little conspiracies orchestrated by Charlotte will soon be her own undoing?"

"Most definitely. It does happen. And it will happen to her."

"Then why warn her, if you believe that?"

"I wanted to threaten her, to make her think about what she's doing and maybe stop."

"And what if she doesn't?"

I shrugged my shoulders, uncertain about what I had said; I just felt the need to say it.

"What happened after Charlotte told you off?"

"Her friends helped her because I gave her a bleeding nose."

"Did she hit you back?"

"No!"

"Then why do you have a black eye, Anna?"

I couldn't lie this time. I had already lied to Dad about my face, but I didn't want to make things worse for myself.

"Did someone else hit you?"

But I didn't answer. I looked away from her gaze, and almost immediately regretted it.

"Stop trying to lie, Anna. You can't cover for someone who is causing you pain."

I sighed in defeat. I couldn't win with this woman.

"Two guys from the football team threw their footballs at my face."

"Well, this is new. The teachers never told me this."

"Please, don't tell them. Those boys will just hurt me more for telling."

"Are you scared, Anna?"

A lump formed in my throat, and tears pricked my eyes. Of course I was scared. They were boys, much bigger and stronger than I was. I didn't want to think about what they would do to me if they found out I got them into trouble.

"What are their names?"

"Miles and Bentley."

Lucia wrote their names down on her notepad and looked at me again.

"So, why aren't you at school today?"

"I have two free periods this morning."

"Shouldn't you be using them for study and not a sleep-in?"

"It's still early and you're here…" I frowned.

I seriously didn't understand this woman.

"Yes, of course. Sometimes I forget what day it is. My job is quite strenuous, you see."

I nodded slowly as if I understood, but I really wasn't paying attention to what she said. She had frustrated me with her stupid question.

"So, why do you think Charlotte did this to you?"

"I don't know; it's a sick game to her. She's cruel and vindictive. She has no reason for anything she does."

"Did you give her a reason to strike you with your most abhorrent insecurity?"

"What do you mean?"

"Well, if you look back, Charlotte is obviously still hurt about what happened at the party. How did she know to attack you with this? How did she know it would be successful vengeance and that it would hurt you?"

"She knows I hate my teeth. She knows I'm jealous because she has a million-dollar smile, and I don't."

"So, she knew this would anger you?"

"Yes."

"And it was successful vengeance?"

"Yes, it upset me… but why are you calling it revenge when I did absolutely nothing to her in the first place?"

"But that's not the way Charlotte sees it."

"Is that the way you see it?"

But there was no answer.

"Anna, we can't always explain why people do things. Sometimes, they don't even know why themselves. But we have to keep an open mind. We need to practice acceptance and tolerance during these difficult times in their lives, no matter what."

"I have to love her even though she makes my life a living hell?"

"Sometimes, that's the only thing you can do."

"But what about my feelings? I'm hurt, I'm angry, and I'm confused. Don't I get some sympathy?"

"Yes, Anna. That's why I'm here."

"No, you're not. You're here to tell me that Charlotte isn't a bad person. You're forcing me to love her even though she does horrible things to me."

"I'm not forcing you to do anything. I'm trying to help you see through this fire that you believe is destroying everything in your life."

"Fire?"

"Yes, Anna. Charlotte is the fire, and right now you're the oxygen that's fuelling the flames."

"Are you saying that I bring these things on myself? That I am the cause of Charlotte's temper?"

"Yes and no."

"Well, what the hell does that mean?"

This lady was driving me mad; she was saying one thing and meaning another. I wasn't even sure if she was on my side to begin with.

"Anna, you have to be the water. You have to keep calm and quiet, flow gently, and the fire will stop. Fire will only burn when it is given oxygen."

My expression was blank; I understood the metaphor, but it wasn't fair.

"You want me to ignore my sister, forget everything she has done to me and will do in the future? But why?"

"She will eventually stop when she sees that she is no longer hurting you."

"You mean when her plans start to fail? And Charlotte's web of lies will unravel and fall apart?"

"Not in that sense. Anna, you give Charlotte the ammunition to hurt you; you let her hurt you."

"How?"

"By letting your insecurities get to you. Charlotte would never have used that photo of you in that way if you weren't so self-conscious about your teeth."

"So, it's my fault? Everything that she does to me is my own fault? And I deserve it because I give her the power to hurt me?"

"No, you do not deserve the things that have happened to you. But yes, you do give her the power to hurt you."

"So, what am I supposed to do? Just let it all go?"

"Yes, let it all fly over your head and don't give a care in the world, or at least don't show that you care. The more you care and lash out, the more the fire will burn you."

I hated to admit it, but her theories made sense. I knew that if you play with fire, you will only get burned, but fire leaves permanent damage that cannot be fixed.

"I suppose I can let it go, what she did to me at school yesterday. But... there is something that I need to tell you, something that Charlotte has done that cannot be forgiven."

"And what is that?"

"I'll be right back."

I disappeared to my bedroom for a few seconds and then returned to the lounge room with the anonymous letter I had found in my locker.

"Someone put this in my locker," I began, handing Lucia the note. "And I think I believe it."

I waited a few minutes as she read over the letter. I wondered if it would change her opinion of Charlotte. I hoped so, anyway.

"Tell me why you believe this person," Lucia, the psychologist, asked.

"Well, as I told you at the hospital, I opened my eyes when Dad found me in the forest of Jenson Park. I saw his hurt expression, the pain in his eyes. But when I looked at Charlotte, I saw nothing but emptiness and a kind of disappointment, like she was upset that I hadn't died. I believe the person who wrote that letter because I truly believe my own sister couldn't care less about me. I know she wishes I had died; I see it in her eyes and on her face. And for her to laugh so hard she had tears in her eyes… well, that's just… sadistic."

"Sadistic?"

"I am her little sister, and the fact that she wishes I were dead is wrong. Sisters are supposed to be kind and caring, loving, and supportive. A normal person would cry and be absolutely devastated, in a state of substantial shock, if their sister were left for dead in the cold and dark. A normal person would help their sister if she were lost, cold, and scared, regardless of any fights they had earlier. A normal person would visit their sister in the hospital after a near-death experience that left her comatose. And my sister did none of those things, so there is nothing normal about Charlotte."

"Does this letter make you feel sad?"

"It's not the letter that makes me feel sad or angry; it's my sister's complete lack of sensitivity."

"Perhaps she was actually crying but felt embarrassed, so she laughed instead."

"Why do you keep doing that?"

"Doing what, Anna?"

"Sticking up for her like she's innocent."

"Why does innocence have anything to do with this whole situation? Or guilt, for that matter?"

"My sister is guilty of a lot of things, leaving me in the cold and dark, for one. If she had picked me up like she said she was going to, I would never have been attacked."

"Anna, I understand that you feel the need to blame…"

"She is partly responsible. I won't sit here and blame the entire thing on her, but that doesn't mean she has no responsibility in my near-death experience."

"Are you angry?"

"Yes."

"Why?" she asked, though it seemed obvious.

"Because you're defending her just like you defend David Hagan! I thought psychologists are supposed to help."

"Am I not helping you, Anna?"

"No, you're making me angry. I thought that was at least obvious to you."

"Once again, Miss Finch, I am trying to help you see why people do these things, but you're turning this into a heated argument."

"It's only an argument because you're trying to make me guess…"

"Think," she corrected, which only made it worse.

"Then bloody tell me why people like Charlotte and David do these things," I shouted.

I was standing over her like a giant, like a bully threatening a small child. But Lucia remained calm, which was strange.

"People like Charlotte and David have their own insecurities, Anna," she started.

She spoke gently and nonchalantly. For a moment, I wondered if I had scared her, but I hadn't. I had won. She gave in to me.

"There are certain things they don't like about themselves, so they take them out on others. Charlotte is bored with herself, tired of being popular and going down the same road she has always taken. She has come to realize that the road she has taken will end. There is life after school, and whether it seems like it or not, nobody cares about popularity or appearances anymore. Charlotte is afraid to enter the real world because all she has is her appearance and her popularity, but we both know those are not the best attributes needed to get a job.

Your sister wishes she were like you because you see beyond the things she strives for. She knows there's more to appearances and popularity, but she doesn't have the perspective you have to see through them. You know there's more to life than surviving the schoolyard. And she's threatened by it. But she also knows that you have better things going for you. You're an artist; you have perspective, focus, and drive. Charlotte does not have these, but it is up to her to find them within herself."

"Charlottes jealous? But that doesn't make sense."

"To you, it doesn't because you see through your own clarity. You don't have to think about the things you do; you just do them. It's like when you pick up a pencil and just draw, a picture creates itself. But at the same time, you could be thinking of something else. Charlotte cannot do this, not without having a good long hard think about it or using a stencil. But even then, she doesn't get it right. It's not simple to her; it's forced. And that's why you don't understand the things she does. You let things go more often than not, but Charlotte doesn't. She takes everything to heart."

"What do you mean by using a stencil?"

"Charlotte will try to be like you, copy you just like you use a stencil to copy a picture, but she won't ever get it right. She cannot be like you, no matter how much she tries because it's the little things that you let go, that Charlotte cannot. She won't ever get the picture right because she doesn't have the perspective that you have; she cannot see through the stencil."

"If that's the case, then why does she treat me the way she does?"

"She knows that if she puts you down, you will not do the things you love because you're hurt. She knows you will fail at school and drop out because she makes it hard for you to cope, but that's when you have to stand up and put on a brave face. Ignore her; avoid her, or smile at her. She will soon self-destruct."

I wasn't sure if I was lost. It all made sense, but then again, it didn't.

"If I don't feed the fire, it will go out."

"Exactly."

"What about David Hagan? What were his reasons for attacking me?"

"David was a very damaged individual. He attacked you because he couldn't attack himself."

"But why did he want to attack himself?"

"He blamed the death of his daughter on himself."

"She died?"

"Anna, David Hagan was part of a murder-suicide."

"I thought you said he was innocent."

"He was. Do you remember what I told you in the hospital?"

"That his ex-wife left, taking his daughter with her, and never letting him see her again. Oh…"

As I spoke, the pieces began to fit together. David's ex-wife had murdered their daughter and then taken her own life, driven by a desire to prevent them from being together. She was ashamed of David and believed she could never have a fulfilling life with him.

"That's horrid. But it still doesn't explain why he attacked me."

"Anna, consider this: David's feelings towards women were deeply conflicted after his ex-wife's actions. He both hated and loved them. He blamed himself for the tragedy and sought to punish himself, but he did so by punishing you."

"He punished me for being a woman?"

"It may be hard to grasp, but minds like David's operate differently. He not only punished you for being a woman but also for being present that night. He wasn't inherently violent, and I don't believe he intended to harm you…"

"But he was blinded by both wrong and right."
I frowned, struggling to understand. How could something be both wrong and right?

"Yes, Anna. But he needed to do something to end his pain."

"You think he attacked me to feel guilty, to have a reason to end his own life? He inflicted pain on me to escape his own suffering?"

"Yes."

I felt overwhelmed. So much of it made sense, yet so much didn't. I just wanted to go back to bed.

"Do you understand what I'm saying about thinking like Charlotte and David? Sometimes, we can't immediately comprehend why they do what they do."

"I think so. But why didn't you just tell me that stuff earlier instead of making me guess?"

"Think," Lucia corrected me again, "Because discovering things on your own are easier to understand."

6

That following Friday, both Year 11 and 12 students sat for their mid-year exams. I had taken a few days off to study, confident that my overall grade would be more than acceptable. Charlotte had been in her usual irritable mood, mouthing off at me whenever she was home. Dad was either swamped with work or passed out drunk on the lounge or in his bedroom. After my conversation with Lucia, I reflected on her advice about being water when Charlotte was fire. I remained calm and quiet, even smiling, which seemed to annoy my sister. It worked for a while, at least until an hour after my exam.

I completed my exam to the best of my ability and, having finished a few minutes early, I felt quite sanguine and content with my efforts. I even smiled to myself, hopeful about my performance. However, my optimism was short-lived as I was summoned to the principal's office. I assumed he wanted to further discuss the incident between my sister and me, but I had already spoken with Principal Williams the day after Lucia visited me.

"Ah, Miss Finch," he began that previous Wednesday, "I'm glad you're here. Dr. Lucia Thorne informed me that two Year 12 boys on the football team were involved in giving you that black eye. It was with great pleasure that I suspended both Miles and Bentley. I have also warned the rest of the team that if they attack you in any way, the entire football team will be disbanded this year. Does that sound fair?"

I was speechless; it was more than fair. Finally, someone had taken action against these relentless bullies. I felt relieved but couldn't shake my concern.

"Are you okay?" he asked.

"Yes, I'm just worried about the repercussions."

"But there are none, Anna."

"Not from you, Mr. Williams."

"Anna, is there more you need to tell me? Should I be concerned?"

"No, I don't think so."

"Are these kids bullying you?"

I didn't answer, but my expression gave me away.

"How about you go home for the day? Don't come in tomorrow either."

"What about my schoolwork?"

"You have an exam on Friday, and there isn't much classwork to catch up on, so take the next few days to study."

"Thank you."

"But there's one other thing, Anna. You did set school property on fire, and you will have to replace it. Do you have any income? Do you have a part-time job?"

"No."

"Then I'll send the bill to your father."

"Do I have to do any community service?"

"Not at this stage. Dr. Thorne has informed me that your sister and her friends were also involved. They have been given a warning."

I sighed in frustration.

"Is something wrong, Miss Finch?"

"No. Can I please leave now?"

"Of course. Chin up, Anna."

I had left the principal's office in a bad mood on Wednesday morning, but everything seemed resolved. As I entered Mr. Williams' office on Friday, an hour after my exam, I felt a wave of concern. I sat across from Mr. Williams, nervously picking at my fingernails and frowning. I expected further punishment for setting the bin on fire, but what happened next was unexpected.

"I gave you two days off school to study, Anna Finch."

"I know, Mr. Williams, and I did."

"Oh? And how do you think you performed on your mid-year exam?"

"I studied diligently on Wednesday and Thursday; I woke up early and stayed up late. I thought I did exceptionally well as I didn't find the exam too difficult."

"Are you going to sit there and lie to my face, Anna Finch?"

"I'm not lying, Mr. Williams. I actually finished a few minutes before the time was up."

"I have no doubt you did, Ms Finch. In fact, it wouldn't have taken you long at all to complete this."

He dropped an exam paper on the desk in front of me, looming over as I read my name and signature on the entry section at the top of the page. I suddenly felt faint as I saw that all my answers had been completely erased, but what disturbed me the most was the profanity scrawled across the entire page in permanent marker. Someone had written a vile insult about Mr. Williams.

"Read aloud what it says, Miss Finch."

I hesitated, "Principal Williams sucks donkey d…"

"Stop there!" he snapped.

"Oh, Principal Williams, I assure you that I did not write this. I swear on my mother's grave. I take school very seriously and completed this exam to the best of my knowledge."

I flicked through the pages of the exam booklet, but the same profanity was scrawled on every page. I looked up at Mr.

Williams and saw a mix of anger and hurt in his eyes. He slumped back in his chair and sighed.

"I am very disappointed in you, Anna."

"But I didn't do this. It's not even my handwriting."

I tried to show him by comparing my name and signature that I had written myself, but it was no use; he didn't believe me.

"My hands are not covered in permanent marker, sir. Look."

I held up my clean, innocent hands. But he shook his head.

"I have no option but to give you a week's detention and community service."

"But I didn't do it, I swear."

"Then who did, Miss Finch?"

"I don't know," I replied softly.

Then I remembered my last visit to the principal's office.

"Miles and Bentley, sir."

"Excuse me?"

"The last time we spoke, Wednesday morning, I told you there would be repercussions because Miles and Bentley were suspended. Do you remember?"

"Of course, I remember. But what are you getting at?"

"It must have been them, Mr. Williams. They're trying to hurt me, get me into trouble because I got them suspended."

"You didn't get anybody suspended, Ms Finch. Miles and Bentley suspended themselves."

"And now they're trying to get me suspended. These are the repercussions about which I was talking. It was them, not me."

"Anna, it was your test paper. I have no option but to punish you for this."

"But that's exactly what they want."

"That's ludicrous."

"Believe me, I know. But it's true."

"Do you have any questions before you leave?"

I sighed. I was going to take the rap, just like they had planned.

"Can I sit the exam again?"

"Yes, but you will have to do it now. They're being sent away this afternoon."

"Can I be supervised?"

He frowned before answering the question.

"If you wish, I'll send Mrs. Malone to keep a thorough eye on you the whole time."

"One other thing, Mr. Williams."

"What's that, Miss Finch?"

"When I'm finished, may I bring my exam paper straight to you?"

"What do you mean?"

"Can I place it on your desk with the others before you send them away?"

"Not before I briefly look over it."

"I just want to make sure it goes straight to you and doesn't wander off into someone else's hands."

He frowned again but this time I saw something different. A kind of smirk, like he believed for a moment that I was innocent.

"Sure."

I took the exam again, feeling quite comfortable with Ms Malone keeping a close eye on me. I wasn't even concerned that she began to stare; at least I knew she was witnessing it, and that's all that mattered. When I had finished, I handed the paper to Ms Malone. She looked it over and smiled, handing it back to me.

"It wasn't me, you know," I started as we walked to the principal's office.

"I know, sweetheart."

I handed the paper to Mr. Williams and watched intently as he skimmed over the answers, ensuring I hadn't missed any questions. He then placed it inside a yellow envelope with the others and sealed it. He then put it inside another envelope, a white one made of plastic bearing the Board of Studies logo.

"I will personally transport this to the post office myself," he said, smiling briefly as he walked out of the office.

"If you are satisfied, Miss Finch, you may go home now," said Ms Malone.

"I'd say so; it's past 4 pm already."

I was a block from my house when Bentley and his mates pulled up in his brother's Hilux with a tray of dirt. It was a twin-cab, which meant room for a few more idiots. I paused as the Ute pulled onto the sidewalk in front of me. Four boys got out and jumped in the back. One of them was Miles. I don't know why I stood to watch; I was intrigued by what they were doing. But I should have run as soon as I saw them pull up.

My heart sank as I watched them pick up clumps of dirt and aim for me. I wanted to run, but my feet were metaphorically glued to the ground. All I could do was shield my face with my arms as they opened fire. Clumps of dirt hit me hard, bruising my entire body. A few large ones struck my face. The clumps exploded upon impact, spraying dirt all through my hair and clothes. I tried to scratch my eyes as they filled with dirt.

I heard an old woman shout out to me and then shout something to the boys, but they didn't stop. More and more clumps of dirt were thrown at my body until someone threw a rock that struck my temple. I fell to the ground, dizziness overcoming me as everything went black.

"The police are on their way," shouted the old woman. "I have your registration plate, young man."

There was a loud screech, and several car doors slammed shut. The boys were leaving. The Hilux screamed down the street and disappeared.

"Are you okay?"

The side of my face was wet with blood and my ears began to ring. I felt faint. I was not okay. My eyes wanted to stay closed, but I fought it. I looked to the old woman who still clutched the phone in her hands. I wondered if she did get the registration plate.

"I'll call the ambulance."

The paramedic checked me over thoroughly, cleaning the cut on my head before applying butterfly stitches. He advised me to go home and take it easy for a few days.

I sat in the gutter while the police questioned the old woman after speaking with me. There wasn't much I could tell them; I had forgotten Bentley's real name and didn't know his brother's name, so I claimed ignorance about the boys' identities. Constable James seemed sceptical; I overheard him telling his partner that it was odd for a group of boys to attack a stranger without reason. I could have provided names and motives, but I chose not to. Dr. Thorne had advised me to be like water, and in this case, Miles, Bentley, and their friends were the fire.

"Are you sure you don't know who they were?" asked Constable James.

"Yes," I lied.

"Will you give us a call if you remember anything else? Or if you recognized any of them?"

He handed me a card with several contact numbers. I nodded as he and his partner climbed into their patrol car. Once the vehicle drove out of sight, I started walking home. My spirits lifted, and I momentarily forgot about the incident. Sitting in my driveway was a shiny red car with a cardboard flap taped to the side that read, "Happy Birthday Anna, Love Dad." I was thrilled. I had gotten my license a few months earlier and was eager to start driving on my own, but Dad hadn't found a suitable car until now.

"Yay!" I squealed, running toward my father as he came out of the house. "Thank you so much, I love it."

I wrapped my arms around him with such enthusiasm that I almost knocked him over. He laughed and handed me the keys.

"Happy Birthday, Anna. Shall we go for a drive?"

"Yes, please!"

I could hardly contain my happiness. I wanted to scream and jump for joy but restrained myself, feeling my head start to throb.

"Wait, what happened to you?"

He frowned and tilted my head to get a better look at my injury. He shook his head.

"It's nothing, Dad, I swear."

"What happened?"

"I fell. You know me, I'm clumsy... and not proud of it."

"Yes, I know you're clumsy, but you've been falling an awful lot lately. Maybe I should make an appointment with the optometrist."

"No, Dad. It's not my eyes."

"Perhaps a brain specialist then?"

"No, I'm fine."

"Well, we're not driving today. We'll see how you are tomorrow; maybe you can drive yourself to school."

"Tomorrow is Saturday, Dad."

"Oh, yes..."

"But maybe I could take you for a drive."

"Yes, well we'll see. I have a lot of work to do this weekend and may not even be home."

It was always one or the other: alcohol or work. My father was only present in my life about 15% of the time, and when he was, it was either overwhelmingly smothering or dreadful. He tended to drink and then become overly emotional, which often manifested as aggression. From a young age, I learned to stay away from his drunken self; even then, I knew it was safer to just stay in my room. When Dad was drunk, he hated me. When he was hungover, he was the sorriest man alive. When he was sober, he tried his hardest to be there for us, often giving us money or buying us things. But mostly, he worked as hard as he could, trying to provide for his small family. I understood that all this was his way of trying to find a void, a moment of peace for his troubled mind. He sought an escape, something to distract him because his mind was tainted with the love and loss of my mother. It was as if he was trying to forget her just long enough to ease the pain and focus on something else. He slaved away at his job, always keeping himself busy, and for a few days, it seemed to work. He was happier, calmer, and somewhat collected. Yet, there always seemed to be a lapse when something reminded him of my mother, or perhaps it was just the realization of why he was working so hard. Whatever the trigger, it didn't matter; the only thing that mattered was that he cared enough to start drinking again, only to forget it all over again.

I wished he would look to other alternatives, like a friend or a psychologist. If I started drinking every time I had a problem, I would undoubtedly become an alcoholic too. But I was not inclined that way. I knew I wasn't old enough to get my own liquor, and although Dad's was always lying around the house, I never felt the urge or the need. It seemed ridiculous to resort to alcohol when faced with a problem. I just didn't see how making oneself blind drunk, with all its incapacities, would solve anything. But solving the problem wasn't what my father was trying to do. He resorted to alcohol as a coping mechanism. He didn't want to forget my mother entirely, perhaps just temporarily, by drinking until he passed out. He loved her too much to let go. I always knew he wasn't strong enough to find another woman, and it was sad. I would have liked a mother figure of some sort.

7

The next morning, I woke up early, eager to take my brand-new car for a drive. I planned to have lunch by the beach with Douglas, as there wasn't much else to do, and it was a beautiful day. I fed the two baby birds I had found during the week; they were starting to grow feathers, and their eyes were almost open. I looked up at the walnut tree from which they had fallen, but their family was nowhere to be seen. It was hard to tell, as I wasn't even sure what type of bird they were.

In the kitchen, I packed a snack bag for the beach, including some treats and a ball for Douglas. I sighed happily to myself, but my mood shifted when I noticed the biggest smirk on Charlotte's face as she walked into the kitchen. I turned away so she wouldn't see me frown. She was up to something; I could feel it.

I went to check if Dad was in his bedroom, but his bed was made. He mustn't have slept here last night, or maybe he had slept on the lounge and left early. Douglas followed me around my bedroom as I packed a change of clothes, brushed my lengthy hair, and applied some makeup. I felt fresh and ready for a beautiful day with my little prince charming; it had been a while since I had spoiled Douglas.

I walked to my car, but as soon as I stepped out the front door, I stopped in my tracks. My mouth hung open in utter shock. Someone had completely trashed my car. The windows were smashed, the doors were dented and spray-painted, and every tire had been slashed to ensure there was no air left in them. I was angry, but sadness overwhelmed me. I had been so looking forward to driving myself to the beach. After one of the worst weeks at school, this was supposed to be my escape. It wasn't fair.

I glanced at Charlotte's perfect, shiny car, and something sparked inside me. If my car had been vandalized by hooligans, why hadn't hers? They were parked on the same street, and Charlotte had been home the entire time. It didn't make sense. I wanted to scream and cry and throw a tantrum like a toddler, but I composed myself. I remembered the look Charlotte had given me just now in the kitchen. It was sheepish yet sly. Charlotte could never keep a straight face. But now it was my turn.

I walked back inside as if I hadn't seen my car yet, maintaining a straight face as I passed Charlotte, who was eating a bowl of cereal in the kitchen.

"What are you doing?" she asked, looking puzzled.

"I forgot something," I lied, keeping my cool as if nothing were wrong.

I wanted to keep Charlotte in the kitchen for as long as possible, making her think I hadn't seen my car yet, and it was working. She was likely waiting around to hear me scream in exasperation, which explained why she was eating breakfast exceptionally slowly that morning. I went into Dad's office, found a pair of scissors, shoved them into my bag, and walked back out, passing the kitchen. Charlotte was smirking again, but I would soon wipe that look off her face.

I acted quickly, first phoning the police and reporting what had happened. I gave them the address and hung up. Nervously, I looked around, but no neighbours were out yet; the street was quiet and empty. I took out the scissors and walked over to Charlotte's pristine car. I stabbed all four tires multiple times to ensure they would deflate completely. I then scratched the side of her car, leaving a big, thick word for her to read as soon as she walked out of the house: "DOG." I couldn't smash the windows as it would be too loud. I wiped the scissors clean of my fingerprints and quickly put them back into my bag. I walked out onto the road and watched as the police car pulled into our street a few blocks down. That was my cue.

I screamed as loud as I could, dropped my bag, and ran up to the door of the house, barging through.

"Charlotte, come quick. Something terrible has happened," I yelled.

She came slowly, still wearing her pyjamas.

"What happened?" she asked half-heartedly, as if she couldn't care less. It was almost a yawn.

I knew she was aware of my car's condition; she had likely asked her football friends to vandalize it in the middle of the night. That's why she acted dumb this morning and got up when I did. She is never in the kitchen eating breakfast when I'm up; she waits until I leave or does it before me, so she doesn't have to look at me. I know how her mind works.

"Someone has trashed our cars," I said quickly, running out onto the lawn.

"What?" she yelled, suddenly wide awake.

She looked at her car and then at mine. She then looked at me with the devil in her eyes and lunged for me. Just as she grabbed my hair and started punching my face, the police pulled up. Both officers leapt out of their car and had Charlotte on the ground within seconds. The smirk had certainly jumped from Charlotte's face to mine. I had gotten even, and there was nothing she could do about it this time.

"Are you okay?" asked one of the officers, Constable O'Riley.

"Yes, I think so."

She examined both cars while the other officer put Charlotte into the back of his patrol car.

"What came over her?"

"I have no idea. She has been strange all morning. I was about to head to the beach for the day when I saw this," I pointed to my car.

"Is your father home?"

"No, he has been at work all night. He doesn't know what happened yet."

"Maybe you should give him a call while I have a chat with my partner."

I called Dad, and he wasn't happy. He couldn't afford to pay for the damages right now, so both Charlotte and I would be without cars for a while. I didn't mind at all; I couldn't miss what I never had, but it was different for Charlotte. She had had her car for over a year. I logged into Facebook while I waited for O'Riley, and to my surprise, there was a video of four people trashing my car. The page was linked to an Anna Finch Hate Page, and the likes and comments were ridiculous. I shook my head as Constable O'Riley came over, frowning.

"Did you find something?" she asked.

"Yes."

I held up my phone and showed her the video. She then walked to the patrol car and returned with an odd device in her hand.

"May I have your phone for a minute? I'd like to extract that; we will run an analysis back at the station and see what comes up."

I handed her my phone and watched intently as she pushed some buttons and entered codes into the small, brick-like machine. She handed back my phone once the machine beeped.

"Did you hear anything last night or early this morning?"

"No, nothing."

"Did you see any lights outside or wake from any strange disturbances?"

"No."

"Okay, well we're going to ask your neighbours a few questions and then we will be on our way. Do you need a lift anywhere?"

"No, I'll catch the bus later. Thank you for asking, though."

"No worries, mate."

"What are you going to do with my sister?"

"Possibly charge her with aggravated assault and intent to harm. We'll keep her at the station for a few hours; it might do her some good. In the meantime, I suggest you stay away from her. Is there anywhere you can go? Grandparents? Aunt or Uncle?"

"No, I don't think so."

"Okay. Well, you will be hearing from us. Have a good day, Ms Finch."

"Thank you, Constable O'Riley."

As the police officer walked across to the neighbours, Richard pulled up in the street and got out of the car. He saw Charlotte sitting in the patrol car and frowned, raising an eyebrow suspiciously as he looked at me.

"Hey."

"Hey."

"Why is your sister under arrest?"

"She attacked me."

"She attacked you? Seriously?"

"Yes, my head is pounding."

"She hit you that hard?"

"No, I was hurt yesterday. Some guys in a Ute showered me with clumps of dirt; one of them threw a rock."

"What the hell, Anna? What is with everybody attacking you?"

"I have a fair idea," I said, glancing at my sister.

"So, who trashed Charlotte's car?"

"The same person who trashed mine, I presume."

"Don't lie to me, Anna. You should know I know you well enough to know whether you lie or not. Plus, I saw the video on Facebook this morning, which is why I am here."

I sighed. He really did know me too well; I couldn't lie to him.

"I trashed her car. I knew she told the boys to trash mine so what is a little pay back? I know she won't confess just to get me into trouble. She never takes any responsibility for her actions."

"Oh, Anna. You shouldn't have. You know it makes you just like her."

"No, it doesn't. I'm nothing like her and never say that again."

"Sorry, just don't do anything stupid like that again."

"I won't."

"You better not. Anyways, what were your plans for today?"

"I was going to take Douglas to the beach, in my new car. But now…nothing I guess."

"I could go for a surf. How about you come with me?"

"Are you sure?"

"Yes, grab your bag and lock the house."

"I won't bring Douglas. There's not much room in your car and I don't want to have to sit him on my lap on the way home, he loves to swim, and I'd rather not smell like wet dog."

"Okay," laughed Richard.

The beach was a picturesque haven; I reclined on the sand, basking in the sun's warm embrace while Richard expertly navigated the waves on his surfboard. His skill was impressive, and I found myself contemplating the idea of requesting a lesson, though my inherent clumsiness made me hesitant. The sun's intensity eventually became overwhelming, prompting me to raise the tall umbrella Richard had thoughtfully provided. His consideration never ceases to amaze me.

"Will you join me for a swim?" he inquired, planting his surfboard firmly in the sand.

"It's not quite warm enough," I replied.

"Come on, it'll be fun. If it's too chilly for little Anna, you can always get out," he teased.

I rose and disrobed, unveiling my modest bikini. Though I had no intention of swimming, preferring instead to relax, Richard's persuasion proved irresistible. He gazed at me for a few moments, scratching his head before turning towards the water. I dashed after him, the scorching sand beneath my feet, but stumbled and plunged into the water with a resounding splash. The icy chill elicited a squeal of both shock and exhilaration. As I regained my footing, Richard tackled me, submerging us both as the waves cascaded over us.

"You're so clumsy, Anna," he chuckled as we both gasped for air.

"Shut up, I really hate that about myself."

"Well, I love it," he laughed.

An awkward silence ensued, leaving me uncertain whether he was sincere or if it was merely a jest.

"Let's have some lunch."

I had to break the silence; I could see that Richard was embarrassed or worried and I couldn't let him suffer.

"Sure, it's way too cold to swim anyway."

We ate lunch in silence, punctuated only by the occasional giggle when we caught each other staring. It was clear that something lingered between us, an unfinished chapter. Our relationship had been perfect, save for my sister's interference.

"I still think about you a lot, Anna," he confessed.

"Me too," I replied, my voice barely above a whisper.

He looked at me as if he wanted to say more, but his phone rang. I watched him converse, searching for words, but his tone suggested he was about to leave, so I remained silent. Our awkward moment hung in the air.

"I have to go; practice is starting early today. Sorry, Anna," he said, ending the call.

"That's okay. I had fun."

"Me too. Thanks for lunch. Would you like me to drop you home?"

"No, thanks. I think I'll stay here for a while. I'll take the bus."

"Okay, well have a good one. I'll see you at school."

"Okay. You too. See you later."

"Bye."

He left, and I was alone on the sand, surrounded by others surfing, fishing, or swimming. A woman played with her young children a few hundred metres down the beach. I watched, admiring her maternal grace. I longed to know what it felt like to have a mother, a loving woman who gives everything without hesitation. But I didn't and never would.

As the sun began to set, the air remained warm. I walked to the water's edge, letting the tide touch my feet. The water was much warmer than it had been earlier. Still unclothed since Richard left, I decided to swim before it got too dark. I swam for about an hour, the sun replaced by the moon and stars. Floating on my back, I let the gentle tide carry me. I was ten metres from shore when I saw the first bus arrive, knowing the next one would be in half an hour. I swam to the beach, gathered my belongings, and headed for the showers.

The showers were individual, hut-like stalls with hooks only on the outside. I placed my bag of clothes on one of the hooks and set the bag of food on the ground. Ensuring my clothes bag was closest to me for easy access, I closed the door and removed my bikini, draping it over the door to dry slightly before packing it away. I turned on the shower, letting the lukewarm water wash over me, cleansing my body of salt and sand. I thoroughly rinsed my hair to prevent it from sticking once dry.

After finishing, I turned off the water and reached into my bag for my beach towel, but my hand met only the wall of the shower hut. The darkness was more profound than I had anticipated, with the streetlight further away. I extended my arm between the top of the door and the ceiling, pressing my armpit against the door, but found only empty hooks. Crouching down, I reached beneath the door, encountering only the bag of food. Standing up, I felt for my bikini on top of the door, but it was gone too.

I rummaged through the bag of food again, retrieving my phone to use its light. My bikini, towel, and clothes bag were nowhere to be seen. Crouching again, I peered beneath the door, waving my phone light around, but saw only the food bag, sand, and grass. Hoping my clothes bag had simply fallen, I searched in vain. Standing up, I looked over the door once more. People were leaving in their cars, and for a fleeting moment, I wished I had gone home with Richard.

A tan middle-aged man walked past the showers with a snorkel and a flashlight. He wore a wetsuit and flippers on his feet.

"Excuse me," I said from inside the shower.

He paused for a moment, looked around and then shook his head.

"Excuse me, sir," I said again, "Over here in the shower."

He turned to face me and laughed.

"Oh, I thought I was hearing things," he said with a grunt.

"Can you please hand me that bag?"

"Sure thing, sweetie."

He picked up the bag and handed it to me, it was the food bag.

"Are there any other bags out there?"

"Nope, just that one."

"Oh, okay. Well, thank you."

"No worries."

I watched him stroll down the beach and into the water, thinking he must live nearby since he didn't bring a towel or a car. I tried to peek over the top of the door, but the gap was too narrow. I listened as the bus pulled up, its engine humming as people got on and off, then drove away. I waited, hoping someone would walk by, but the silence was unbroken; no footsteps echoed on the path. I called out, but there was no response. I was naked in the shower, my bag stolen, and soon the buses would stop running. I was stranded.

I took out my phone, but it died just as I dialled dad's number. My luck was running out. I waited another half hour for the next bus, but it didn't stop. I couldn't fathom why someone would steal my clothes and bikini. It didn't make sense, unless it was someone I knew.

"Somebody," I started, "Anybody. Please, help me."

I paused but heard nothing.

"I'm stranded...somebody stole my things. Hello?"

"Hello?"

I frowned and looked out over the door; it was the man I saw earlier with the snorkel.

"Why are you still in there, kid?"

I sighed. I wanted help, but not from a complete stranger.

"Someone stole my clothes and...I'm kind of stranded."

"I see."

"Do you have a phone that I could borrow?"

"I do, but it's up at my house. I don't suppose..."

"No, it's okay; I'll find a way home."

"I don't think I can let you do that."

"What do you mean?"

"You'll get hurt, love."

"But you don't know me…"

"That doesn't mean I care any less about the safety of a young girl. I have daughters, you know."

"I'll be fine on my own, thank you."

I was grateful that he wanted to help but walking to this stranger's house, naked, wasn't something I was about to do. I wasn't even comfortable talking to him through a door.

"Look, someone is on their way. Thank you for your generosity but I'll be fine," I lied.

"Suit yourself," he grumbled, walking away.

I was alone again, with no one on their way and no one knowing where I was. Richard would assume I got home safely, and Dad was either still at work or passed out drunk at home. And Charlotte… hell, Charlotte probably did this. The more I thought about it, the more certain I became that she had something to do with this. Another half hour passed before I saw anyone. A girl walked straight toward the shower.

"Hello? Stranded girl?"

"Um, yes?"

"My dad sent me down here; said you needed some help."

She pushed a plastic bag under the door. I took out a pair of underwear and a summer dress which was quite cute.

"I didn't pack a bra because I didn't know what size you were, but you don't really need a bra with that dress."

The girl was friendly and didn't seem fazed by my nakedness. Although it was somewhat awkward for me, her kindness in offering me clothes was a relief. A towel would have sufficed, but her gesture was much appreciated.

"So, if you don't mind me asking, how did this happen?" she inquired.

"I was showering, and when I went to get dressed, my bag was gone. I think someone stole it," I explained.

"That's awful. People can be so cruel," she responded sympathetically.

Once dressed, I stepped out of the shower and paused, seeing the girl standing before me. Her reaction mirrored mine; she was just as shocked to see me as I was to see her. We were both speechless.

"Mirandah..." I said, recognizing her.

"Anna..." she replied, equally stunned.

8

It was strange. Without Charlotte, Mirandah seemed like a genuinely nice person, a stark contrast to the puppet she usually appeared to be. I wanted to talk to her, to see if she could truly be different without my sister's influence. After all, Charlotte was the one who gave all the orders. But I could never understand why people followed her instead of making their own decisions.

"I didn't know you lived right on the beach," I began.

"Yeah, it's beautiful," she replied softly.

"Do you surf?" I asked.

"No, I'm actually afraid of the water," she admitted.

"Afraid of the water? Can't you swim?"

"I can swim; it's what's in the water that scares me."

"Oh, you mean… sharks."

It was a hard word to say, especially in front of her, given her involvement with Charlotte's cruel printouts. She gave me an awkward look, as if she could read my mind. I wondered if the image from the printouts flashed in her mind when I mentioned sharks.

"You know that was all Charlotte..." she started awkwardly, "And I'm sorry I ever had anything to do with it."

"Then why did you? Why do you have anything to do with my sister? You, of all people, know how horrible she is to me."

It was the truth and saying it to Mirandah almost brought me to tears.

"I know, Anna. She is a horrible person, and I hate that I'm friends with her..."

"Then why are you, Mirandah?"

"I don't know. I guess I'm scared of her. She is a bit of a psychopath."

"That's the understatement of the century," I replied.

She laughed. And then it was silent again.

"A lot of people don't understand her, I mean, she's your sister and yet she does these horrible things to you."

"What do you mean a lot of people? How can you speak for others?"

"Anna, we all talk about her," she replied, "Sometimes, it's all we ever talk about."

"Why?"

"We feel sorry for you...and what happened that night."

"Charlotte says I deserved it..."

"I know. But you didn't."

"She doesn't care, you know. She wishes I were dead."

"I'm sorry to say but I know that too. She goes on about you trying to steal her limelight or something. It's completely mental."

I shook my head. It was typical Charlotte; it didn't surprise me although it felt strange coming from Mirandah. And this girl was supposed to be one of my sister's best friends.

"Did you really attack her this morning?"

"What? No. And how do you know about that?"

"Facebook. Charlotte wrote some ridiculous status this morning about being attacked by her own sister… claimed she was really hurt and sad about it. A lot of people took pity on her."

"Christ," I sighed, "That's not what happened at all."

"It's okay, I believe you, Anna. She's always threatening to bash you. I was quite surprised the other day when you hit her. She went on about it for days. She kept saying the sun was in her eyes, otherwise she would have hit you back."

"She has anger issues."

"That she does," Mirandah agreed, "I remember when you were in year 7 and had just eaten a banana with lunch. You threw the peel toward the bin but missed and accidentally got Charlotte. She went ape. Do you remember?"

"Of course, Mirandah. It was traumatizing."

"The thing was, yelling just wasn't enough for her. She had to grab you by the hair and drag you across the playground. She really stepped out of line when she thumped your head against that brick wall."

"I didn't think anybody saw that," I frowned as the memories came flooding back.

Mirandah looked to the ground for a moment as if deep in thought.

"Has it always been like that?"

"Unfortunately," I sighed.

"Why don't you ever try and stop it? Like stand up for yourself. You did alright the other day."

"Because I know she's stronger than me... and she's irrational, and scary."

"Do you really believe she might be insane?"

"I don't know."

And that was the truth. I didn't know if my sister was seriously mentally ill or if she was just taking her suffering out on me.

"She was always mean to me when we were younger, but I was too young to really notice or care. I tolerated her. The only reason we grew apart was because I was old enough to see who she really is. I became old enough to see her true colours and know that I didn't have to be treated like trash anymore, even though I still am. But do you know what I mean?"

"Yeah, I do. You're so strong, Anna. Has anyone ever told you that?"

I shook my head. I didn't know if I believed it myself.

"Do you really hate me?" I asked her.

"No, Anna. I never hated you. Before I knew Charlotte was psycho, I always thought you were weird because you were quiet. But anybody who is alone is quiet."

"Well, that's true."

"I don't know," she sighed, "I guess I just wanted to fit in. Charlotte is popular and I thought everybody loved her. Well, they did for a while. But nothing lasts forever."

"Honestly, if this hadn't happened to me today, would you have ever spoken to me?"

"Honestly? Well, I guess not. But things have a strange way of working themselves out."

"So, now what? What's going to happen when we go back to school on Monday? Are you going to treat me like trash just because Charlotte says to?"

There was a long silence before she replied.

"I don't know, Anna."

"Yeah, well neither do I."

I was angry and confused, but mostly I just wanted to cry. It wasn't fair. Mirandah didn't even like Charlotte, yet she stuck by her for the sake of popularity. She wasn't willing to risk her own reputation to do the right thing. It felt completely immoral. But I guess she was nothing more than a sheep.

"I called you a taxi, it should be here soon."

I nodded.

"Well, I have to go. My dinner is waiting. Bye Anna."

"Bye."

When I entered the house, it was quiet except for my father's snoring, which came from his bedroom. The darkness made it difficult to navigate, and I stumbled my way to my room. Douglas was already asleep on my bed, indicating someone had opened my door. I frowned, but assumed it was Dad letting Douglas in.

I considered checking on the baby birds, but they were silent, likely asleep, so I decided not to disturb them. I kept their cardboard box under my bed, just as my mother had done when she was younger. The thought made me smile, feeling a connection to her, even though I only knew her through stories.

That Monday, I had detention all morning, a punishment for the exam paper incident and for setting the bin on fire. While I accepted the consequence for starting the fire, taking the blame for someone else's stupidity was infuriating.

When I opened my locker, I was met with a revolting sight: old, moldy food everywhere. Rotten tomatoes, nearly black, and eggs, along with other unidentifiable items, filled my locker with the foulest odour imaginable. Tears welled up in my eyes, and bile rose in my throat as I cleaned it out. I managed to wipe some of my schoolbooks, but others had to be thrown away.

While cleaning, I found an envelope with "Put these on your wall" scrawled across the front in permanent marker. Inside were four photos that made me almost vomit. Someone had taken the baby birds I had saved and fed them to their dogs while they were still alive. One photo showed a baby bird suspended by its leg, attached to a piece of fishing line, hovering over a dog's open mouth. Another showed the dog eating the bird, its tiny legs and feathers protruding from the bloodstained mouth. It was cruel and sickening.

I realized I had forgotten to check on the baby birds that morning in my rush to get to school. They had been oddly quiet Saturday night but were fine when I checked on them in the morning, eating and drinking well. I had planned to free them in a few weeks. I was home all-day Sunday, except for a long walk with Douglas in the afternoon. Whoever did this must have entered my room when I wasn't home, and the only person who knew about the baby birds was Charlotte, having heard them cheep occasionally.

The bell rang, signalling it was time for detention. I cleaned the rest of my locker as quickly as I could and ran to the detention room, stuffing the photographs into my bag. I was five minutes late, but the teacher didn't seem to care; she was engrossed in a book, *Heartbeat* by Danielle Steel.

"Great novel, I once read it in four days," I said as I passed her.

She raised an eyebrow but didn't say a word. I sat at the back of the class and spread my workbooks out on the table. If I was going to spend a week in detention, I wasn't going to waste my time. Having missed a lot of work while I was in a coma, now was the perfect opportunity to catch up.

Two hours slipped by quickly, and I hadn't even noticed that a different teacher was now at the front of the class, or that five other students had joined me in detention. The room was no longer as quiet, which bothered me because I couldn't concentrate. I rolled my eyes and sighed, slumping in my seat, and leaning my head on the desk. The teacher was engrossed in his phone, laughing, and frowning at the screen. At least he was entertained. I glanced at the clock; it was almost time for recess. As I started to pack up my books, I noticed something written on the desk.

I looked closer and read my sister's name in a rather disturbing sentence. As I continued reading, there were more: "Charlotte Finch's legs open on weekends. Charlotte Finch never gives up the D. Charlotte Finch is a bully. Charlotte Finch thinks everybody loves her. Charlotte Finch is a stuck-up cow. I hate C Finch. Charlotte Finch is a liar. Charlotte Finch is ugly. Is cruel. Is mean. Is the devil. I wish Charlotte Finch would grow wings and fly away."

I realized I wasn't the only one who saw through my sister's sadistic ways. It seemed many people didn't like her at all. Charlotte Finch wasn't as popular as she thought she was. I kept reading until I came across my name: "Anna Finch is a free-spirited, beautiful person and I love her." It was heartening to read that someone loved me and thought I was beautiful, but with hundreds of kids in my school, I doubted I would ever find out who wrote it.

The bell rang for recess, and I walked past my locker on the way to the cafeteria. I emptied it out and left the door open to air it out. The rotten food was more of an inconvenience than anything else; my real concern was the fate of the baby birds I had rescued. I knew the twisted person responsible was my sister, as no one else knew about the birds in the cardboard box under my bed.

I sat alone in the cafeteria for no more than five minutes before Clara joined me. She glanced at the photos spread out on the table in front of me.

"No wonder you're not eating," she said, screwing up her nose.

"I'm not hungry; I'm trying to figure out who did this."

Clara took a photograph and studied it for a moment, looking carefully at the dog in the picture.

"I've seen this dog before, it's Marcus Jacobs' from year 12."

"Does he go to this school? I've never heard that name before."

"No, he goes to West Bridge. But that's definitely his dog; I've seen him walk it a thousand times."

"Charlotte must be screwing him too."

"Why do you say that?"

"The baby birds in the photos," I started, "I saved them a few days ago. I had them in a box under my bed; I was going to let them go once they were strong enough. Charlotte is the only person that knew about them."

"Are you sure these are the same birds? I mean, I know it's cruel, but it could be a coincidence."

"Clara, these photographs were in *my* locker."

"What are you going to do about it?"

"Nothing," I sighed, "There's nothing I can do. I don't think the police would take me seriously, plus there's no face in the photographs and that may as well be anybody's dog."

"I suppose you're right."

Clara munched on an apple as I glanced over at Charlotte's table. The only unusual thing was Mirandah's expression; her head was down, and she looked on the verge of tears. Charlotte, engrossed in conversation with Lauren, Abigail, Alyssa, and Ruth, didn't notice—or care.

I scanned the room for Richard, but he was nowhere to be seen. Luke, Sebastian, and Thomas sat together, chatting casually. Sebastian caught my eye and smiled, a silent greeting. I turned back to Clara, who was absorbed in her phone, the half-eaten apple in her other hand.

"I wonder what's wrong with Mirandah," I said softly, I didn't think Clara heard me, but she replied.

"Charlotte slept with the boy she's been crushing on for years."

"What? Poor Mirandah."

"Why do you feel sorry for her? She's such a bitch to you."

"She wasn't on the weekend," I replied, glancing toward Mirandah again.

"What do you mean? What happened on the weekend?"

"I was at the beach with Richard, and he had to leave for practice early. I stayed, had a swim, and then had a shower. When I reached for my bag to get dressed, it was gone. So was my bikini."

"You were naked?"

"Yes, long story short, I was stranded in the shower butt-naked and Mirandah kind of saved me. Although she didn't know it was me until I came out of the shower. But she gave me some clothes first."

"Why didn't you just call your dad? Or me?"

I paused for a moment; I was surprised to think that Clara would have been willing to help me, and in such a situation.

"My phone died," I replied.

"So, what happened when you got out of the shower?

"We talked."

"About what?"

"Charlotte and how horrible she is."

"Mirandah admitted that Charlotte was horrible?"

"Yes."

"And she still hangs with her? That doesn't make sense."

"Believe me, I know."

I glanced toward Charlotte's table again, but Mirandah and Danielle had disappeared.

"I saw that your car was trashed, Charlotte is telling everybody that you did it."

"What?"

My attention was suddenly drawn completely away from Mirandah.

"What is she saying?" I pushed.

"She says that you trashed her car and then trashed your own so you wouldn't be suspect. But it doesn't make sense, only your car was posted on Facebook."

I shook my head. I wasn't surprised. I couldn't tell Clara the truth, I didn't trust her enough. It still felt a little awkward that she was even talking to me again, which pushed me to ask her.

"Can I ask you something?"

"Sure," she replied, but the answer wasn't so convincing. It was almost as if she was afraid of what I might ask her.

"Did you really believe those lies Charlotte told you? The lies that ruined our friendship?"

There was another awkward silence, and I knew she was hesitating. She looked guilty when she spoke.

"Anna, I'm sorry. I was angry and didn't know what to think. Charlotte was so persuasive, pretending to be there for me. I thought she was my friend, but she just wanted to hurt you. A few weeks after it happened, she discarded me like trash. That's when I realized it wasn't true, and I felt like such a fool for believing her. You were so hurt, I thought you hated me, so I stayed away. I guess I never came back until now. I didn't deserve to have you as my best friend anymore."

Clara's words hung in the air, filled with regret and sorrow. I could see the sincerity in her eyes, and it made me reflect on the pain and confusion we both had endured. It was a lot to process, but maybe this was a step towards healing.

"It's strange how things work out..."

I couldn't bring myself to say that I forgave her; it just didn't feel right. It took her a few weeks to realize how wrong she was to believe Charlotte, yet she let me think for almost a year that she still believed my sister's lies. For almost a year, she didn't talk to me, and for almost a year, I beat myself up over it. Usually, I didn't let things like this get to me, but everything felt so heavy at the moment. So many things were happening at once, and for a moment, I just wanted peace.

Clara's apology was sincere, but the hurt ran deep. It was hard to reconcile the friend I once knew with the person who had abandoned me. I needed time to process everything, to find a way to move forward. Maybe, in time, I could find it in my heart to forgive her, but for now, I just needed to focus on getting through each day.

I stood up and walked out.

9

I got home early that afternoon; I just had to get away from school. Talking to Clara had been overwhelming. I was angry at her for not telling me sooner that she didn't believe Charlotte's lies. If she had, things might have been resolved by now. I missed my best friend more than anything. She had been my rock through everything, and it hurt to watch her leave so abruptly. We were like sisters, always close, and seeing her walk away with my sister that day tore my world apart. Even though I was sobbing uncontrollably, she never looked back. I loved her so much. But now, our friendship was tainted with denial and misunderstood hatred. It felt like a lie.

After getting home, I cleaned up the kitchen after Charlotte cooked dinner. It drove me insane how she made such a mess and then walked away carelessly, as if she had the right to leave her mess for someone else to clean. She did this often, not just in the kitchen. I scrubbed the fat off the stove and walls, scraping it off with a plastic spatula. Charlotte never cleaned when I cooked; she never lifted a finger. She would leave her plate out and sometimes chew food until it was mush and then spit it on her plate, not because she didn't like it or was full, but out of spite. I was yet to do it back, but I wasn't that immature.

Dad left after I finished cleaning, heading back to the office for another endless night of work. I didn't mind; a good movie was premiering on television, and I thought I'd watch it. But when I walked into the lounge room, Charlotte had the whole lounge to herself and clutched the remote, ensuring no one could change the channel.

"There's nothing on," she complained to herself.

"Can I have the remote then, please? There's something I want to watch and it's starting now."

But she pretended not to hear me, changing the channel to an old German film with subtitles. I knew she hated those, but she did it out of spite. Rolling my eyes, I walked back into the kitchen and decided to make a cup of tea. Searching through the mugs from where I sat proved difficult and quite foolish, as one fell from the cupboard and smashed on the bench.

"Halfwit," I heard Charlotte say from the lounge room.

I felt like snapping back at her but busied myself with cleaning up the broken glass. As I finished, I noticed something on the bench: a cigarette. It must have been hidden in the mug, the end burnt as if someone had lit it and then quickly put it out. I frowned, my eyes wandering to the lounge room. It had to be Charlotte; it certainly wasn't me, and Dad wouldn't need to hide it from us.

I examined the cigarette, feeling strange holding it. I saw a lighter near the microwave, snatched it without thinking, and quietly went outside. Douglas greeted me with a wagging tail, sniffing the air curiously. I put the cigarette between my lips and lit it. My first drag made me cough violently, but I tried again, breathing in slowly and deeply, letting the smoke spiral inside my lungs. I exhaled and took another drag, feeling different—loose and calm. For a moment, I understood why people smoked. I might have even liked it. But as that thought crossed my mind, I put it out and threw it away. The idea of becoming addicted so quickly scared me, and I kicked myself for even trying it. I knew it was bad for me and felt guilty for having just a few drags. Paranoia set in, and I thought about the damage that single cigarette could have done if I had smoked all of it.

I went back inside and washed my hands thoroughly. As I put the lighter back, I found a whole box of cigarettes stashed behind the microwave. I was about to reach for them when Charlotte walked into the kitchen. She frowned, looked me up and down, then sniffed the air and folded her arms.

"Have you been smoking?"

"No," I lied.

"Yes, you have, I can smell it. Wait until dad finds out about this."

"You will only be dobbing yourself in Charlotte, they're yours anyway."

"Pfft, no they aren't."

"Then you won't mind if I do this."

I reached for the cigarette packet and pulled out a handful and quickly snapped them all in half. They didn't even have time to hit the ground when Charlotte lunged toward me. I was taken by surprise and gasped for air as she pushed me hard up against the bench. I felt her shirt in my hands as I grabbed hold of her. She had a handful of my hair in one hand and closed fist in the other. She punched me in the side of the head once and then twice. I grasped hold of her hair too, my other hand prying at the hand that was on my head. My hand moved from her hair to her throat, and I squeezed as hard as I could, but my grip slipped as she kept punching me repeatedly in the face. I felt blood drip from my nose, but it didn't hurt. Adrenalin coursed through me as I pushed her away from me and into the cupboard in the kitchen. I punched her in the face three times before she yelled and pushed me hard, spinning and pulling me toward her again.

Douglas was barking and scratching vigorously at the door. I knew he wanted to get inside and rip Charlotte to shreds and he would given the chance. He was very protective of me.

I felt hair rip from my scalp as Charlotte twisted my head, making it easier for her to punch me. I thought about going limp and letting her hit me, it wouldn't look good with her current record. But Charlotte was likely to never stop, she would probably kill me. And those thoughts could not have been truer in that one moment as I saw her free hand reach for the knife block on the bench closest to her. I punched her in the stomach as hard as I could, simultaneously pushing her hard against the bench. She clutched her stomach and for a second, I was free. Without thinking I ran to my bedroom but as I reached my door I paused and looked over my shoulder, for a second, I felt bad for hitting my sister and a part of me wanted to go and see if she was okay, but I knew she was fine as she hurdled down the hallway toward me with a knife in hand.

I slammed my door shut and fumbled for the lock, locking it shut just as I felt her reach the doorknob. My heart was pounding. She banged on the door with her fists, kicking it and scratching at the doorknob.

"Let me in so I can bash your head in," she yelled.

"Not likely," I whispered.

"Come on, Anna. Open the freaking door."

"You have a knife, Charlotte; think about what you're doing."

"Oh, I am thinking. I have been thinking about this for a long time."

Thinking about what? Murdering me? Slitting my throat open and ending me? Lucia was dead wrong; my sister is ill. My heart sank as she stopped thumping. I put my ear to the door, but she was no longer in the hallway. I wanted to open the door to make sure, but a part of me was screaming *no*. The sound of screeching chalkboard filled my ears and the scene from a horror film filled my mind. Charlotte was outside. She tapped on the window with the knife.

"Anna, come here, please," she called from my window.

I leapt onto my bed and opened my curtains. I wanted to see her; I wanted to keep an eye on her.

"Open your window, Anna," she said slowly, but it was strange, it was like she was possessed or something.

"No!"

"Open the freaking window," she yelled.

My window faced into the street and all I could think was why the neighbours hadn't heard her yet.

"Leave me alone before you do something stupid and end up in prison for the rest of your life."

She looked at me with an odd expression. I couldn't tell if it were hatred or sorrow. But then it changed, she just stared at me with black empty eyes.

"Charlotte, you need help. You're sick."

"Open this window, Anna. Open it now!"

I was too scared to move. Opening the window was out of the question; I wasn't that foolish. It would have been a death sentence. She thumped on the glass, her fist clenched around the knife handle. My face was wet with tears—I hadn't even realized I was crying. She pounded the window again, this time cracking the glass. A twisted smile spread across her face as she glanced at the damage. Charlotte looked at me, raising the knife as if preparing to stab. She struck the window repeatedly, each blow more forceful than the last, until the glass shattered. My heart sank. Panic set in as she began pulling the broken shards away, readying herself to climb through. I pulled out my phone and dialled for the police. She looked up once she heard me speaking.

"Hello, my name is Anna Finch. I'm being attacked by my sister; I'm locked in my room, and I fear for my life. She has a knife. Please come quickly."

As I gave the address to the officer on the phone, Charlotte stared at me in shock. I couldn't tell if she was stunned that I had called the police or if she finally realized the extent of her madness. She backed away from the window, but her eyes never left mine. A part of me wanted to hug her; she looked so sad. I soon found myself sobbing uncontrollably. I was sorry that Charlotte had lost it, sorry that I was scared of her, and sorry that I had to call the police. I cried and shook violently until the police arrived. By then, Charlotte was gone.

The police came and went. I gave my statement, and they helped me cover the broken window with a thick sheet of fiberglass I found in the shed. They tried to call Dad, but he didn't answer; he was probably too busy or passed out on the lounge in his office. I held Douglas all night; he licked my tears away, trying to comfort me. I didn't understand why I was so upset; I hated my sister, and I knew that would never change after what had just happened.

"How are you feeling?" asked Lucia when she visited early the next morning.

"Tired."

"Well, that's because you cried all night. Crying is good; it means you can now move on."

"Move on? How am I meant to move on from this?"

"You have to forgive your sister."

"Those that threaten murder and then physically try to end someone else's life are things that are not taken lightly. Things like that are not easily forgiven. I will forever be hurt by Charlotte's actions."

"But you must remember that she had a reason."

"She tried to lie but I found her out, she got mad..."

"You fuelled the fire, Anna."

"Oh, screw your theories. I've had enough of you. You don't know what goes on until you've been in my shoes and witnessed all of this firsthand."

"I understand," she said calmly.

"No, you can't possibly understand."

"Anna, I have degrees in this sort of thing…"

"Education and experience are totally different things. And until you have some form of support for me, I wish to end these visits."

"But I am supporting you, Anna."

"No, you're not. You're telling me that my sister is not a bad person, but she is. She's the devil. Now please leave."

I wasn't in the mood for Lucia that day. She always seemed so negative, always defending Charlotte, and it hurt. It felt like she was calling me a liar.

I arrived at school early that morning, as early as I could after Lucia left. I tried to cover the bruises on my face with generous amounts of makeup, but some things even makeup can't hide. People stared at me. Clara raised her eyebrows and widened her eyes when she saw my face, as did Kim and Lucy.

"Oh my god, Anna. What happened?" asked Clara.

"Did your psycho sister do that to you?" asked Kim.

"Yeah, I haven't seen her yet today," said Lucy.

"It' still early, she could turn up," I replied, "And yeah, we had a fight last night."

"Over what?" asked Lucy.

"I broke a few of her cigarettes…"

"Oh, boy."

"Dad doesn't know yet, and I don't think he will be very happy with the window."

"What happened to the window?" pushed Kim.

"We had a fight, I got away and then she tried banging down my door. Then she tried at my window, smashed it trying to get in at me."

I said it quite softly so as not to advertise it. I don't know why, naming and shaming Charlotte would probably be good for her, but I just wasn't the attention seeker she was.

"You know what's going to happen now?" said Clara.

"She's going to turn the story around to make me look bad."

"Yeah, but it won't work, Anna. Look at you," said Kim.

I found it strange that Kim and Lucy wanted to comfort me, but maybe they were just sick of Charlotte too. I already knew people hated her; the graffiti on the desk in detention said so. Charlotte wasn't as perfect as people thought she was. The cracks were showing.   "Anna, oh my god, what happened?"

Richard walked straight up to me, embracing me in a tight hug. He held me close, then stepped back to look at my face. Luke, Sebastian, and Thomas stood by.

"Do I need to ask?" he said.

"No, you already know."

"Christ. She needs help," he said, shaking his head. "She can't keep doing this to you."

"I kind of provoked her."

"It doesn't matter. She should know better."

"She had a knife," I whispered, so only he could hear.

He was too shocked to say anything, just staring at me. After a while, he shook his head and rubbed my arm, trying to comfort me.

"You're tough, Anna," Thomas said, playfully punching my shoulder as he walked past with Luke and Sebastian.

I turned to Richard, who looked like he still wanted some sort of explanation for what happened between my sister and me. But I didn't want to explain.

"So, how was practice the other day?" I asked, trying to change the subject.

"Fine," he sighed, frowning at me.

I didn't want to think about Charlotte with the knife. I had spent the whole night avoiding nightmares. It still sent shivers down my spine to know that my sister could have slit my throat or stabbed me repeatedly if I hadn't gotten away when I did. It was hard to believe that she actually had a knife and intended to use it, especially when she said she had thought about doing it for a long time. My sister was undoubtedly and irrevocably insane.

10

At lunch, I was surprised to find a group of people at my table—a group I could now call friends. I sat quietly, taking it all in. Clara, Lucy, and Kim chatted happily while Sebastian, Luke, and Thomas had their own conversation. Richard sat and stared at me. I blushed when I finally felt his gaze, and he laughed as my cheeks grew scarlet. I wasn't sure if there was something between us yet, but there was definitely something growing. It was strange; we had history. But this was different. It was new and exciting.

Just when I had erased any thoughts of my sister, she walked into the cafeteria. I frowned as I saw her, and Clara, Kim, and Lucy followed my gaze, their expressions mirroring mine.

"I thought you said you didn't really hit her back," Clara said.

"Three times. In the face. But it wasn't that hard. There's no way I could have done that to her."

Charlotte walked into the cafeteria with more bruises than a giraffe has spots. There was a purple ring around her neck, like someone had strangled her. I remembered exactly what happened, and I knew I didn't hit her that hard.

"She's trying to get me into trouble," I spat. "I didn't freaking hit her that hard."

"Calm down, Anna," Richard said.

"No, the stupid whore has done that to herself."

I was just as shocked as everyone else at the table to hear those words escape my mouth. I never used foul language like that, but I was more than angry.

"What did you tell the police, Anna?"

"The truth," I said softly, still watching Charlotte as she sat at a table with her friends.

"Anna, what did you tell them?" pushed Richard.

"I told them that I broke her cigarettes and that she lunged at me. I told them she attacked me first, and that's the absolute truth."

"Did you choke her?"

"I tried to, but I only had one hand."

"Where was the other?"

"Trying to pry her hand out of my hair, or on her head. I can't remember."

The whole table looked at Charlotte. We studied her face from afar. She had bruises on both sides of her face, a black eye, a fat lip, a cut in her eyebrow and multiple bruises on her arms. The panicked expression on my face caused her to smile as she glanced toward me. But something else happened at that moment. Charlotte's attention was stolen by Mirandah who stood up and spoke quite violently to her. They were too far away for us to hear anything, but they soon had the attention of the whole cafeteria.

"Mirandah must have confronted her," said Kim.

"About what?" asked Thomas.

"She slept with Corey Jones," said Lucy.

"Yeah, and?" Thomas pushed.

"She's been in love with him since the seventh grade."

We watched as Mirandah shouted something and pointed toward me. It caught me off guard, but Charlotte continued to glare at her. Danielle started to drag her away, but Mirandah burst into tears and ran outside. The cafeteria stared at Charlotte.

"What was that about?" asked Luke.

"Yeah, why did she point at you, Anna?" asked Richard.

I sighed. But when I spoke, it was directly to Richard.

"The other day when you left me at the beach, something happened, and Mirandah saved me from a lifetime of embarrassment."

"What happened?" he pushed; an eyebrow raised.

"I was showering after my swim, and somebody stole my clothes, towel, and bikini. Mirandah brought me some clothes and called a taxi."

"How did she know that you were at the beach?"

"She lives nearby, and her dad passed me, offered to help but I said no. And then Mirandah turned up."

"Why didn't you call me?" asked Richard, his expression hurt.

"My phone died. And you were at practice."

"Screw practice. I would have come and helped you, Anna."

I smiled; I was grateful that he cared.

"Actually," started Luke, "It might be possible that Charlotte had something to do with that."

"I don't doubt that."

"No, I'm serious. She wrote a status on Facebook, it said 'There may be streakers at the beach tonight. Make sure your camera has a flash.' Or something like that."

"I wonder why Mirandah never said anything."

"She probably unfriended her like a lot of people," suggested Kim, "I know I have."

"Man, she's a total bitch," interrupted Lucy who was staring intently at her mobile phone screen.

"What is it, Lucy?"

"Charlotte posted a photo earlier this morning, a mug shot saying she was brutally bashed by her sister. You should see the comments, especially from Lauren, Abigail, and Alyssa."

"I don't think I want to," I said quietly.

I knew the extent of some people's cruelty; I had seen enough of it on the hate pages made specifically to hurt me. I knew Lauren, Abigail, and Alyssa were close to Charlotte, and I had a feeling that one of them was behind the Anna Finch hate pages. I knew they were never my friends, and I was glad I had unfriended them days ago. They only ever posted selfies with their cleavage on display, soaking up every ounce of male attention they could get. They were materialistic, high-maintenance girls, and I was happy not to be associated with them.

"Why haven't we seen you in class, Anna?" asked Sebastian.

"She has a week's detention for setting that bin on fire," laughed Luke.

"Yeah, she used my lighter," added Thomas.

"Why did you do that anyway?" asked Lucy.

"I was trying to destroy those printouts that Charlotte made. You know, the ones with the shark."

"Oh, yeah. I didn't see the point in that. It wasn't even funny. What point was she trying to make?" asked Lucy again.

"That she has perfectly straight teeth and I don't."

"Your teeth are fine, Anna. You're actually a lot prettier than her."

"Thanks, Kim. But it's still a major insecurity of mine."

"Don't let it be," started Luke. "If she knows what upsets you, she will always use it against you."

"Yeah, and you can fix your teeth if you're that concerned," added Thomas. "Get braces."

"Tom's right, Anna. You can fix your teeth, but you can't fix how ugly Charlotte is on the inside," Clara stated.

"Years of therapy might help," said Richard under his breath.

They were all right, but it didn't change the fact that I had a few more days of detention left. And that's exactly where I went when the bell rang.

After school, I observed Richard at practice. He requested that I stay so he could drive me home. He insisted on staying over for the next few days to ensure my safety, fearing that Charlotte might attempt to harm me again. I was still awaiting a response from the police and contemplated whether I should inform them that Charlotte had appeared at school today.

When we arrived at my house, Richard's phone rang. He took the call in his car while I went inside. I let an eager Douglas out, who had been waiting at the back door, his tail wagging excitedly at the sight of me. He immediately ran onto the lawn. It frustrated me that Charlotte couldn't even let him outside. I knew it was out of spite, but Douglas was an innocent animal. Charlotte didn't care if he made a mess inside; she knew I would have to clean it up, regardless of how long it had been there. However, Douglas was well-trained and always held it in, though I knew it wasn't good for his bladder.

"Why couldn't you let him outside?" I asked her as I walked into the kitchen.

Lauren, Abigail, and Alyssa glared at me as they stood next to my sister.

"Because he's not my freaking dog," she grunted.

I rolled my eyes and as I went to walk past them, I was grabbed from behind and spun around. Lauren and Abigail both had hold of my arms, twisting one behind my back and holding the other out in front of me.

"Let me go, what the hell are you doing?" I said loudly.

Alyssa reached her arms around me from behind and put her hands over my mouth so I wouldn't scream. My eyes widened in disbelief and pure fright as Charlotte got out the blender. Surely not, I thought. My sister hooked the blender up to the electricity and put a punnet of strawberries inside the jug. She held down the lid and turned it on. I watched as the blade turned the fruit to puree. But I dreaded what was coming next as she emptied the fruit juice into a glass and set up the blender once more. She turned it on full and I watched as the razor-sharp blades spun furiously.

I felt myself being pushed and pulled forward, toward the blender. Lauren took my right arm tight, Abigail my left outstretched. I struggled to get free. I tried to pull my arm away from the blender, but they hung on tight and dragged my hand into the jug, inches away from the blade. I screamed but the sound was muffled by the hands over my mouth. Douglas barked ferociously outside, scratching on the window, and jumping up and down. My arm and shoulder hurt from struggling to pull free. Tears streamed down my face as I feared the torture that was coming. The hands that were covering my mouth soon became wet with my tears, slipping from my mouth. I bit down as hard as I could, drawing blood. Alyssa yelped. I screamed as loud as I could. I screamed for help. I screamed for Richard. My fingers were so close to the rotating blade, I felt the movement of the air right at my fingertips. My lungs felt like they were going to burst from screaming so loud.

"Anna?" Richard called, running inside.

Charlotte's eyes widened, her mouth hanging open in shock. She let go of my arm, turned off the blender with a trembling hand, and bolted to her bedroom. The three girls trailed after her, their footsteps echoing in the suddenly silent kitchen. I collapsed into a corner, tucking my hands away as I curled into a ball. The scent of freshly blended fruit lingered in the air, a stark contrast to the turmoil inside me. I wanted Richard, but he wasn't there. His angry voice boomed from the bedroom, each word a dagger to my heart.

"What the hell were you thinking? All of you? You could have seriously hurt her, and I don't mean a few cuts and bruises. You better stop this bullshit, Charlotte; she's your little sister."

There was a long pause before he spoke again.

"You're all as mental as each other, and don't think the police won't hear about this Charlotte, because I'll be on my way in just a moment. As for you girls, do you seriously want bad names for yourselves? Hang with her and you're going to do just that."

"We only wanted to scare her," said Alyssa.

"You all make me sick," he spat.

He stormed into the kitchen; eyes blazing. With a swift motion, he ripped the blender from the wall and hurled it across the room. The crash echoed, shards scattering across the floor. He ran his fingers through his curly hair, his frustration palpable. Bending down, he scooped me up into his arms. My heart raced as he carried me out to his car, the cold night air hitting my face.

"Did they hurt you?"

"No," I whispered.

"Do you want me to grab Douglas? There's no way in hell I'm letting you stay here tonight."

"Please."

The sooner Richard left, the sooner he was back with Douglas in his arms. He passed the chubby pup to me as he climbed into the driver's seat. Douglas's tail wagged furiously; his joy infectious. He always loved Richard, and the feeling was mutual. As Douglas licked my tears away, his warm, soft fur brushed against my cheek. He sat and stared at me with those big, understanding eyes once I stopped crying. He always knew when I was upset, and his presence was a balm to my aching heart.

"Your sister is a something else," he said once we arrived at his house, "Maybe you shouldn't stay there for the next few days."

Richard put Douglas outside with his Labrador, Jupiter. Despite both being male, Jupiter, with his age and gentle nature, never minded the company of other animals. Richard then cooked me dinner, the aroma of spices filling the kitchen, and drew me a bath with too many bubbles and a few scented candles. It was lovely, the warm water soothing my frazzled nerves.

When I entered his bedroom wrapped in a towel, he glanced at me briefly before walking out, giving me privacy. I found some clothes I had left here months ago when we were still together; he had neatly placed them at the end of the bed. I was surprised they still fit, a small comfort in the midst of chaos. Richard pulled out a mattress and placed it beside his bed, insisting I take the bed while he sprawled out on the mattress with a sigh.

"How are you?" he asked quietly.

"Pretty fantastic right now," I replied, smiling a sleepy smile.

"Good. Do you promise to stay that way?"

"I promise. Just for you."

He smiled and closed his eyes.

I couldn't get comfortable that night. I tossed and turned, rearranging my pillows until finally, I slipped into the deepest sleep. I dreamt of dark shadows and heavy, looming trees in a thick forest. The sound of snapping twigs echoed around me. Black clouds surrounded the moon, swallowing it whole. The air was cold, the breeze brisk. Goosebumps prickled my skin, and the hair on my arms stood on end. I was cold, but something else lingered. I could see my breath escaping in thick white rasps, but that wasn't it. I felt a presence. I wasn't alone.

A scream pierced the silence, a cry for help. I couldn't tell from which direction it came, but somebody was calling out to me, somebody needed my help. I found myself running, my legs moving swiftly, my feet pounding the ground. Darkness enveloped me until the moon emerged, casting silver light on the tall trees lining my path. I ran until I couldn't feel my feet anymore. The ground disappeared beneath me, and I fell rapidly through the darkness. I tried to scream, but no sound came out.

I fell for what felt like an eternity. Below, a forest loomed closer. The air became sharp and ice-cold, like pins and needles on my skin, tiny knives cutting and jabbing at my face. The forest faded, revealing a small clearing of black dirt. In the centre lay something small and fragile—a person, face down in the dirt. I was there in an instant, standing over the body. I reached out and turned it over. I gasped as I saw my own face, sad and silent. Cold, white, and stiff. My black, empty eyes stared back at me in pain, searching for something.

Slowly, I turned my head to the left. A tall, large figure stood beside me, a man, but he had no face. David Hagan, I thought. He stared down at me, tilting his head in confusion. I looked back at my own lifeless body on the cold, black earth.

But the face had changed. It was no longer me. It was Charlotte.

Charlotte lay stiff and cold on the ground, staring up at me for help. I glanced beside myself again but found that I was standing alone. I looked back at Charlotte. Tears streamed down my face. I touched my cheek, wiping away a tear, but when I glanced at my hand, it was covered in blood. I frowned and looked back at my sister. She was covered in blood, and I had blood on my hands. Her eyes were fixed, black and empty. She was lifeless and pale. She was dead.

I glanced down at my hands again. My eyes widened as I saw the knife Charlotte had taken from the kitchen, tipped with thick, red blood. My heart raced, and beads of sweat formed on my brow. I tried to scream, but nothing came out.

I sat up in bed, my eyes flying open. My breathing was rapid, and I was drenched in sweat. I threw the sheets off, startling Richard, who sat up on the mattress, looking dopey and tired.

"Are you okay?" he yawned, rubbing his eyes.

I shook my head, unable to speak.

"Would you like me to join you for some comfort?" he asked gently.

I nodded, feeling foolish for my inability to speak, just like in the nightmare when no sound came out. Exhaustion weighed heavily on me as I lay down again, trying to relax my trembling body.

"Relax, Anna. It's okay. I'm here," Richard whispered softly, his voice a soothing balm.

I closed my eyes, but the image of Charlotte covered in blood haunted me. Richard wrapped his strong arms around me, and the terrifying vision began to fade. His warmth and presence made me feel safe. I was safe.

11

That Thursday, I sat in the same seat in detention, the one I had occupied Monday, Tuesday, and Wednesday. As I skimmed over the words carved into the desk, I noticed a new sentence that hadn't been there before: "Charlotte's web of lies won't last forever." The letters were etched inside a spider's web, with a long single line stretching the full length of the table. I traced it with my finger, following it until I found the most disturbing carving. At the end of the thread was a tiny body, a noose around its stick-like neck. Beside it, another sentence sent shivers down my spine: "Death be Charlotte Finch."

Detention ended quickly that day, though I didn't get any work done. I couldn't stop thinking about the desk. People were getting tired of Charlotte, but I couldn't believe anyone would want her dead. I walked out into the corridor, hoping to find Richard. He didn't want me staying at home with Charlotte. As I turned the corner toward my locker, I ran into Andie Driscoll.

"Sorry, Anna," she said calmly, turning to walk away but pausing suddenly.

"It's okay, Andie," I reassured her.

"Oh," she laughed, "No, Anna. I wanted to ask if I'll see you Friday night at the party?"

"Party?"

"At your house?" she asked, dumbfounded.

I raised an eyebrow, having no idea about what she was talking. It then occurred to me that it had something to do with Charlotte.

"Your sister said you're throwing a party," Andie continued, "On Friday night, at your house. Everyone was invited."

I paused, realizing Dad must be going away for a work meeting; otherwise, Charlotte would never throw a party.

"My party, you say?"

"Yeah! She said, 'Anna's throwing a party, and everyone is invited.'"

"Oh yeah," I played along. "See you there."

I smiled and walked quickly toward my locker. Charlotte was up to something as usual. As I put my books away, my phone vibrated. It was Richard.

"Meet me across the football field in 10," the text message read.

I frowned; he had told me to wait at the school entrance until he finished practice, but I guessed he was running late. I walked outside and started toward the football field. This part of the school was always empty, kind of eerie. The bell had rung, and students were leaving. Football practice was always Tuesday and Thursday last period, often continuing well after school ended. As I walked across the field, a strange feeling settled in the pit of my stomach. I had felt it before, but every time I looked over my shoulder, nobody was there. I tried to remember if Dr. Thorne had mentioned something about the stages of paranoia, but nothing came to mind. I took out my phone, but there were no new messages from Richard.

As I looked up, I saw a large group of football boys coming toward me. I knew I could ask one of them where Richard was, but as I scanned the group, I only saw the older boys who were friends with Charlotte. The hair on the back of my neck stood on end when one of them pointed at me. I took out my phone again, scanning the deserted playground. I quickly dialled Richard's number, pausing in the middle of the field.

"Hey," he answered, "Where are you?"

"I got your text; you said meet me across the field," I replied in a panic.

"Anna, I never sent you a text. I said meet me at the entrance of the school. I've been waiting here for half an hour; we finished practice early."

"You texted me, Richard. I have the text message on my phone."

"No, I didn't Anna. Where are you? We'll come meet you."

"Whose we?"

"Luke, Seb and Thomas."

"Okay, I'm on the football field."

As I hung up the phone, I turned to see the large group of footballers closing in on me. Their heads were down, eyes fixed on me as they strode forward.

"Hey Finch," one of them called, "Come over here for a sec."

I didn't reply. Instead, a sudden urge to run surged through me. The second my feet started pounding the grass, so did theirs. They charged across the field like a stampede of bulls. My petite legs were no match for their strength. They surrounded me, dragging me into the centre of their large circle. I gasped as one wrenched my backpack off my shoulder and another shoved me hard in the back.

"Leave me alone," I growled, striking out with my fists.

"Help me, help me," one of them squealed mockingly.

"Get off me," I yelled as someone gripped the back of my neck. "Let me go!"

"Oh, please let me go," another teased, raising his voice in a high-pitched tone.

They closed in around me, pushing and pulling me like a rag doll. My head spun with dizziness.

"Leave me alone, you mongrels," I snapped.

I fought back with my fists, but as I struck one in the face, the retaliation was swift. A blow to the side of my head and another to my stomach sent me to the ground. I tried to scream as someone pushed my face into the grass, muffling my plea.

"Help me, help me," one teased, pretending to have his way.

They laughed and cheered, mocking the actions of David Hagan. Fully clothed bodies pressed against mine, mimicking my pleas. Tears spilled from my eyes, and my body ached. I strained my neck, managing to free my mouth from the grass. I screamed as loud as I could. Through the many legs surrounding me, I saw three figures racing toward me, cursing and yelling.

"Get off her," yelled Sebastian, flying into the crowd and punching anyone in his way.

Luke forced his way in, kicking and striking the footballers. Then came Thomas and Richard, full of rage. The heavy weight lifted from my body as the large mass of boys broke out into a brawl. Four boys from the year beneath me— Sam, Michael, Peter, and Adrian—pelted into the group, swinging fists at the footballers.

I sat sore and shaking with fear, watching as one by one, each footballer fell to the ground or ran away wounded. The brawl wasn't over until Coach Cartwright showed up, pulling them apart and yelling at the top of his lungs.

"Break it up, break it up!" he yelled.

He stood back, looking at the bruised, bloodied faces of his team, utterly disgusted.

"What the hell do you think you're doing?" he boomed.

But nobody answered. And I wasn't surprised.

"Someone better explain to me what the hell is going on before I cut the entire team."

His eyes shifted toward me for a moment, and I saw the dumbfounded realization on his face. He walked toward me and helped me off the ground, but still, there was no answer from anybody.

"Anybody care to explain why they felt the need to torment this poor girl? She's been through quite enough," said the coach.

I was a little shocked to hear the words escape his mouth, and it made me wonder if the faculty had discussed the incident that took place in Jenson Park a few months earlier.

"Bentley will tell you," said Richard.

The coach looked to Bentley and raised his eyebrows, expecting an explanation. But the meathead stood with his lips pursed and his head held high.

"If this arrogant prick doesn't own up to this, then I quit," snapped Richard.

"Well Bentley, do you have anything to say?" pushed the coach.

"No sir!" replied Bentley.

Without hesitation, Richard walked toward me, picked up my belongings, and escorted me across the field toward the entrance of the school. A few moments later, I turned to see Luke, Sebastian, and Thomas not far behind us.

"You didn't have to quit," I whispered to Richard.

"It's okay; I'd rather not play with those arseholes anymore anyway."

"I'm sorry."

"It's not your fault, Anna."

It might not have been, but it felt like it.

"Can I have your phone, please?" he asked.

I handed him my phone and watched intently as he went through my messages. He paused suddenly, a small frown turning into the tiniest smile I had ever seen.

"You put XX's after my name?" he asked, looking down at me.

I was suddenly quite embarrassed. "Yes."

"Why?"

"It's been like that since we dated…" I lied.

"But I've changed my number since then," he pushed.

"Yeah," I paused, thinking of an escape, "I just edited the number…not the name."

But he didn't reply. Instead, he smiled to himself; he knew I was lying.

"Well, there's your problem," he said finally.

"What?"

"Someone has been into your phone and saved a number under my name," he replied. "See?"

He showed me my contacts list, displaying two contacts with the name Richard. One titled 'Richard xx,' the other 'Richard.'

"Someone isn't as bright as they think they are," he laughed.

"Who do you think did it?"

"Charlotte, I'd say."

It wouldn't have surprised me if she did do it.

"Do you have anything important on tomorrow?"

"Do you mean at school?"

"Yeah, I had an idea," he started, turning to face the boys as they came up behind us. "You guys want to ditch school tomorrow and hang out at the beach club?"

He walked backward as he spoke to them, staying close by my side.

"Yeah, sounds good to me," replied Thomas.

"Yeah, I have three free periods tomorrow anyway," said Luke. "Screw math class."

"And practice. Those losers can suck it. Coach only has Bentley to blame," said Sebastian.

"Did you guys quit too?"

They all nodded at once, but I couldn't help but feel like it was my entire fault. The expression on my face gave it away too.

"Don't feel bad Anna, those boys are dogs, and I don't play with dogs," said Sebastian.

"A little extra work on the field won't hurt them," laughed Luke.

"So, how about it? Beach club tomorrow?" continued Richard.

"Sounds like a plan. Aren't you throwing a party, Anna?" asked Thomas.

"Apparently I am."

"What do you mean apparently? You either are or you aren't," laughed Sebastian.

"Well, there will be a party at my house, but I won't be there."

"Why would you throw a party and not be there?"

"She's not throwing a party," Richard interrupted, "Her idiot sister told everybody she is."

"So, Charlotte is actually throwing the party?" pushed Luke.

"Yep!"

"Ha-ha this is going on Facebook," laughed Thomas.

The small group walked in silence as Thomas updated his Facebook status. Richard and Anna walked toward the car as the others turned the corner and continued down the street.

"See you guys at the beach tomorrow," yelled Richard.

Sebastian mumbled in agreement as Luke raised his arm in the air to wave goodbye, saluting a raised thumb regarding tomorrow. The three of them disappeared down the street as Anna and Richard climbed into the car.

"I think you better start carting around an icepack," Richard said once pulling out into the street.

"And why is that?"

"Because you constantly need one lately."

"Yeah, but in actual fact I shouldn't be needing one at all."

"I know, I was joking around. Do you remember who hit you?"

"No, unfortunately. Why?"

"I thought we could go give a statement."

"I have had enough of the police, and they don't do any good anyway."

"Do they know that these guys were the ones that showered you with rocks?"

"They were clumps of dirt, only one of them threw a rock…"

"That's not the point, Anna."

"I know…and no, they don't."

There was a moment's pause before he continued.

"You didn't tell them that you knew who they were, did you?"

But I didn't reply. Richard knew me well enough to know when I was lying.

"Why are you so afraid to tell them?" he sighed in frustration.

"Because it won't do any good, Richard, it'll just make things worse for me."

"But you have the opportunity to get them into serious trouble, which is what they deserve because they're all guilty. Every single one of them."

I didn't reply, but I knew every word he spoke was the truth. The car ride was silent the rest of the way home.

12

The next day, we met the boys at the Harrington beach club. It was a beautiful day to swim or surf. I bought a lemonade and sat beneath Richard's umbrella on the warm sand. Around noon, the beach club staff started handing out menus for lunch. The Harrington was the best beach club in Bridge, serving meals wherever you sat. Of course, you had to be a member, and Sebastian's parents practically owned the club, so we were always welcome.

"I'll have a light garden salad with lemon juice," I ordered.

As I finished my lunch, I looked up to see Mirandah and Danielle walking toward me. Their faces wore odd expressions—one of pity, the other of guilt. They hung their heads and looked up at me through long eyelashes. If they had been dogs, their tails would have been between their legs. I felt sorry for Mirandah, given the recent betrayal by my sister and Mirandah's lifelong crush. Charlotte had broken the friend code and truly broken Mirandah's heart. But these girls were still cowards, sheep following the flock master, Charlotte Finch. But was she still the leader?

"Hi, Anna," they greeted simultaneously, almost like weird twins.

"Hi."

"What are you doing over here all alone?" Mirandah asked.

I frowned; I wasn't alone. I looked toward the boys in the surf, and both girls followed my gaze.

"Oh, I see," said Mirandah.

"Why aren't you at school?" I asked.

"We didn't feel like going today," Mirandah started. "Well, we did go, but hardly anybody in our year was there."

"Oh, I wonder why?" I pretended to care.

"Not sure, but the football team has been cut this year. The boys are pretty pissed."

"How pissed?"

"Well, they keep saying they're 'Gunna get 'em good.'"

I frowned again. I didn't know if this was good or bad. It was comforting that someone had actually done something, but it also wasn't. I didn't want to think about what those boys might do to me now. My heart raced, and the hair on the back of my neck stood on end. My near-death experience in Jenson Park suddenly came flooding back. Beads of sweat formed on my brow, and my breathing became rapid. Twelve or so boys against me, all strong and masculine. They had surrounded me yesterday, but the thought of them attacking me again was sickening. What if I didn't have the boys to protect me next time? These thoughts raced over and over in my mind. My stomach churned, and bile rose to my mouth.

"Anna are you okay?" asked Mirandah, dragging me back to reality.

"Yeah," I lied, "I think I just ate too quickly."

"Okay. Well, we're going for a swim. See you later."

I stood from my beach towel, a thousand thoughts racing through my mind. The warm sand shifted under my feet, and the salty breeze brushed against my skin. One day, I would have to go back home; I couldn't live at Richard's forever. Dad would start asking questions, and the police weren't doing anything to protect me. Apart from charging Charlotte and threatening an ADVO, which would be useless. Charlotte didn't abide by the law, or any rule enforced on her. She was ignorant and arrogant. If only they could put her in a gaol cell for a night to scare her, maybe then she would understand and start behaving. Who was I kidding? She wouldn't last one hour in prison; she would get herself shot. But maybe that wouldn't be such a bad thing.

I remembered the desk in detention—somebody else wanted her dead. I paused and shook my head. I couldn't believe I was thinking like this. I didn't need to kill her; I just needed to scare her. Maybe then she would get the message and leave me alone.

"Hey Anna," called a voice from across the beach.

I looked up to see Clara walking toward me with Lucy and Kim. I was quite popular today.

"Is everybody ditching school for the beach today?" I asked, frowning to myself as I thought this was a private beach, members only.

"Looks like it," she laughed.

"Why waste a beautiful day indoors?" added Kim.

"So, what are you doing later?" I asked.

"Well, we're not going to the party, if that's what you mean."

"And why is that?"

"Because Charlotte will be there, no offence Anna."

"None taken," I laughed, "I'm not even going."

"But it's your party, isn't it?" asked Lucy, which I found odd because she rarely spoke at all.

"No, it isn't my party. Charlotte just told everybody that."

Kim frowned and raised an eyebrow.

"Charlotte is weird," she said flatly, disappearing from Clara's side.

I watched as she ran off toward the surf, leaping into some guy's arms and kissing him passionately.

"Who is that?" I asked Clara, who followed my gaze.

"Her new boyfriend, they've been dating secretly for months. So, how are things between you and Richard?"

Her smile was contagious. I blushed as I thought of my night with Richard. Clara's eyes grew inquisitive as she caught my expression.

"Tell me," she pushed, "It's obvious you're both still into each other."

"Why do you say that? Has he said something?"

"No, he hasn't stopped staring at you since I got here."

She glanced toward the water where we both saw Richard sitting on his surfboard beside Sebastian. They watched us intently as the waves rolled beneath them, their conversation seemingly serious. The sun glinted off the water, casting a warm glow on their faces.

"We stayed up late talking and laughing and…fooling around," I started, keeping my eyes on Richard as I spoke. "Even after a year, I can't help but still be madly in love with him."

"I knew it," Clara gasped, grinning from ear to ear. "You should have never broken up anyway. You were like the cutest couple in the entire school."

As I processed Clara's words, it occurred to me why Charlotte went to so much trouble to break up Richard and me. She was jealous because people thought we were cute, and she had nobody. I then realized that she had done the same thing to ruin my friendship with Clara.

"Yeah," I replied, still staring at Richard.

I could have started to talk about my sister, but the thought of her made me mad, so I changed the subject.

"Seeing as we're talking about boys," I started, "How's your man?"

She looked to me and sighed, sitting down on my beach towel.

"I'm not sure if you can call him that anymore."

"Why? You were seeing each other, weren't you?"

"Yeah, but he wants space now."

"Space? He lives three hours from you, isn't that enough space?"

"I don't know anymore."

"What do you mean?"

"Well, it's kind of strange…it changes. When I'm with him he spoils me absolutely rotten, takes me places and buys me things. When I'm with him everything is perfect. But when I come back home…it's not. It's different."

"Different? How so?"

"He speaks to me different. It's not so 'lovey dovey', and then he says he wants to take things slow. I don't understand because I thought it already was slow…we haven't even made it official yet. Anyway, I asked him if he wanted to do it all. Like, see me and stuff…"

"Yeah. What did he say?"

"He said he didn't know…"

"What?"

"He said if something happened…he wouldn't care where it left us."

"Walk away, Clara. Clearly, he is just stringing you along."

I knew at that moment Clara was hurt. She really liked this guy, and he was feeding her bullshit. Tears rolled down her cheeks as she hung her head to the ground.

"I can't…I mean I'm sick of feeling like shit, but I can't walk away. Not when I keep thinking of all the good times we have had."

"Do you love him?"

"I think so, but love isn't meant to leave you heartbroken."

"Leave him, Clara. He's not worth your tears. Have you spoken to him about this? Have you told him about your feelings?"

"He knows. I have tried to end it so many times, but he gets angry and says he doesn't want me to leave…so then I don't. I don't know Anna; I guess I just want to see what happens."

"What did he say when you told him you love him?"

"He doesn't believe me…"

"Did he tell you if he had any feelings for you?"

"Once, but not since everything has changed."

"Do you think there may be another girl?"

"There's heaps…apparently."

"What do you mean?"

"Our last fight, he said he has heaps of girls lined up…and told me not to feel special and that I'm not the only one."

I could see at that point anger was building inside of Clara. And it was building inside of me too.

"No! That's not on. What a creep. What a freaking loser. Leave, Clara. You deserve so much better. You deserve someone who will be afraid to lose you. Someone who would do anything to be with you and want to see how you are every day."

"I know and I want someone like that," she sobbed.

"Tell him you're leaving. When was the last time you spoke?"

"Three weeks ago."

I raised my eyebrows. This guy had probably already been with at least five other women in that time. He sounded a lot like Charlotte.

"Then just leave it. Walk away without him knowing. He will soon realise that he's lost you."

"He will lose his temper again…"

"Ignore him. If he tries to call you or texts you, ignore it. Don't give him the time of day, Clara. You will find somebody, and he will love you no matter what."

Clara sat silently for a moment, wiping away her tears. She then leapt toward me, wrapping her arms around me. She held me so tight I could barely breathe but I felt obligated to stay once I felt her body begin to convulse. She sobbed heavily.

"I'm so sorry, Anna. I should have never doubted you. I was wrong to believe Charlotte," she sobbed, "Even after all this time you still care about me."

I pried her off me, keeping her at arm's length while I looked to her.

"Don't be silly, Clara. You were my best friend, and I will always care for you."

"I will never believe your sister's psychotic lies again!"

"That's good," I laughed.

I knew then that Clara's tears were truly meant for me. I wasn't angry with her anymore, she needed me, and I needed her. We sat on the sand together for the rest of the day, reminiscing the days before Charlotte screwed up our friendship. As the sun started to set, I checked my Facebook to discover that my newsfeed had been flooded with updates and photos. It was 8pm, the party had started 2hours ago.

"There is over one-hundred check-ins at my house for the party," I said to Clara.

"Wow, that's a lot of people. And your house isn't that big."

"I should tell dad, but then she will get everyone to say that it's my party and I will be to blame."

"She's such a scheme artist."

I didn't have to mention her name and Clara knew I was referring to Charlotte. I shook my head in disgust.

"At least Douglas isn't there to be tormented."

"Where is he?"

"At Richard's, I've been staying there the last few nights; he won't let me stay at home with Charlotte."

"Why? What'd she do this time?"

I sighed before answering. I was sick of every conversation being about Charlotte.

"Her and her friends grabbed me…tried to mess my hand up with a blender…"

"What the actual f… Did you tell the police?"

"No, they wouldn't do anything anyway."

"You need surveillance cameras at your house! Before she actually kills you."

"I need protection."

"What like a bodyguard?"

But I shook my head. I didn't want to tell Clara what was really going on in my head. I wasn't sure myself.

"Time to go?" interrupted Richard as he walked toward us.

"Don't they do dinner anymore?" I asked, forcing another topic.

"No, not since that man drowned here one night after closing," replied Thomas.

"What man?"

"His name was Jeremy Pitcher. He was a drunk."

"What happened?" I pushed.

"Well, he had dinner here and a few drinks. They closed at 10pm and he decided to go for a swim, but nobody was around."

"He was too drunk to swim," added Luke, "The owners found his body on the beach the next morning. There was a massive lawsuit and everything."

"Now they have a curfew at 8pm but they don't serve dinner, just lunch," said Sebastian.

"That doesn't make sense."

"Oh yeah, it's screwed up alright. But it always takes one stupid idiot to ruin it for the rest of us."

"Hey Clara," said Richard, "Not at Anna's wicked party?" he joked.

"No…sorry Anna," she replied, glancing toward me with a grin.

"Ha ha, what a nutter," said Luke, looking at his phone screen, but his smile suddenly faded, "Anna, you should see this."

Thomas and Sebastian both had their phones out, there expressions similar to Luke's.

"What?"

"There's a video on Facebook…the mongrel football dogs are trashing your bedroom."

I grabbed the phone off Thomas and watched as the football boys did indeed trash my bedroom. I watched as they ripped the photographs off my wall, tipped my bed upside down, smashed my lamp and began throwing things around my room.

"Oh my god!" I gasped, as one of the boys emptied my closet into a steel drum and set it alight.

I watched as my bedroom filled with smoke and the video was over. I handed Thomas his phone, sat down on my beach towel and closed my eyes.

"Can you see their faces?" asked Richard.

"Yep!" said Luke, watching the video again, "Bentley, Miles, Roger, Phillips and…some other guy I've never seen before."

Sebastian studied the face on Luke's screen.

"That's Colin Murphy, the guy that was done for drugs a few months ago. I didn't think he would be out of gaol yet."

"Right, that's five of them. Let's go," said Richard.

"Where are we going?"

"Police station!"

13

We followed the police to my house. The street was completely blocked with cars, their headlights casting eerie shadows. On my front lawn was a steel drum, its contents ablaze. The flames danced wildly, sending sparks into the night sky. Surrounding it was a group of people who did not attend my school. The acrid smell of burning filled the air, mingling with the distant sound of sirens.

As the police car pulled up as close as it could, one of the officers stepped out, a phone to her ear. My heart pounded in my chest, a mix of fear and confusion swirling inside me. What was happening? Why were these people here? The sight of the fire and the crowd made my stomach churn. I glanced at Richard, who looked equally bewildered.

"She's calling the tow truck company," laughed Luke, "All of these cars will be towed."

We watched as Constable O'Riley retrieved two yellow car boots from the back of the police car, handing one to her partner and proceeding to put the other on the tyre of the closest car to us. The other officer walked to a car that was furthest away, locking the boot to its back tyre. Constable O'Riley then came to my window.

"Anna, may I ask you to remain in this car for your own safety?"

"Yes!"

We watched as she then walked to the police car, spoke on her radio, and then proceeded to walk to the house with her partner.

"Why did they do that?" I asked the boys from my window.

Their car was parked adjacent to Richard's, the windows down so we could talk to each other.

"The two cars with the boots are the only two that will allow any of the others out, they're blocking the rest," said Richard.

"In a few minutes, loads of people will be running from your house once they see the police turn up. They will try to get into their cars and drive away..."

"But they won't be able to," interrupted Thomas, laughing.

"It's about to get really hectic," said Luke, pointing toward the officers.

We watched as Constable O'Riley drew a taser from her belt, as did her partner. They walked slowly toward the group of people around the fire. One person looked up from the fire and bolted, as did the others.

"PIGS!" one yelled, sprinting into the house.

Red and blue flashing lights sped toward the back of our car, two police units pulling up behind us. The officers leapt from their vehicles and ran toward the house, their hands grasping batons, guns, and tasers. People fled from my house, sprinting in every direction. I watched as three officers went inside.

"We're streaking," yelled one very drunk, naked boy, running past our cars and into the darkness of the street. Two girls followed him, also naked.

As I sat quietly beside Richard in the car, my phone rang. It was Dr. Thorne.

"Hello," I answered.

"Anna, hi. It's Dr. Thorne. How are you?"

"Fine, thanks."

"Is it okay if we have a chat?"

"I'm actually busy right now, and it is late…"

"Yes, it is late, but we haven't had a meeting in a while."

It's been a few days.

"How about Sunday?"

"That suits me fine, at your house?"

"No, how about we meet for lunch," I suggested.

I didn't know what state my house was in, and I didn't have the energy to explain it to my psychologist.

"A public meeting, are you sure? You won't lose your temper?"

My blood boiled at the words, but I had to prove to this lady that I wasn't the psycho my sister was.

"A public meeting is fine," I answered with a smile behind my voice.

I wondered if she could sense the sarcasm as I didn't want to meet with her at all. I wanted her off my phone and out of my life.

"Okay, see you Sunday. 12pm. Murdoch's, okay?"

"Fine!" I tried to sound cheerful, but I truly disliked this woman.

Richard frowned at me. I hung up the phone.

"Who was that?"

"My shrink."

"Oh, you have a shrink?"

"Unfortunately."

"Is she any good?"

"She's a pain in the arse. I don't need a freaking psychologist. Charlotte does."

"Yeah, and some happy pills," Thomas laughed from the other car.

I sighed. Now everybody knew I was seeing a shrink.

"What did I miss?" I asked.

"They must have a wagon up the other end of the street because they just escorted that Murphy bloke out in handcuffs," said Sebastian.

"Any sign of Charlotte?"

"Nope! I think she ran for it too."

Thomas and Sebastian ducked inside the darkness of the car as two police officers walked past our vehicles with three boys in handcuffs. One of them I recognized as Bentley. The expression on his face proved that he was far from happy. The blood on his shirt told me he either resisted arrest or was in a fight with somebody else. Either of the two didn't surprise me; he was an arrogant meathead. I couldn't help but grin as he was placed in the police car.

"Finally!" I whispered.

"Yeah, now you can tell the police everything that twit has done to you," said Richard, putting a hand on my lap to comfort me.

My phone rang again. This time it was Constable O'Riley.

"Anna, it's Constable O'Riley. Could you please ask your boyfriend to escort you to the house? It's safe to come in now."

"Yes. Do you have Charlotte?"

"No, officers are doing their best to track her down, but it seems she has gotten away once again."

"Okay. I'll be over in a minute."

I hung up the phone and looked to Richard.

"She said we can go in now."

As I held Richard's hand and followed him into the house, I could already feel the dread in my stomach. The acrid smell of smoke lingered in the air, and the ground felt uneven beneath my feet. I knew whatever mess there was, I would be the one to clean it up. I didn't want to think of the trouble I would be in with Dad. And then I wondered if the police had called my father at all.

I walked into the lounge room, which was littered with trash. One of the police officers I hadn't met guided me toward my bedroom. I walked down the hallway, gasping as I saw my door hanging on a single hinge. The word 'whore' was scrawled in red spray paint. Richard held my hand tighter. I stepped over broken pieces of wood, which I could only assume were from my dresser. As I turned the corner into my bedroom, I saw my dresser in a million pieces, thanks to the axe lying in the centre of the room. Every photograph had been ripped off the wall, replaced with the word 'freak,' also written in red spray paint.

I looked at my upturned bed; the mattress had been slashed with a knife, its springs spilling out from gaping holes. Tears welled up in my eyes as I saw everything I owned, broken, tainted, or burnt, scattered around my bedroom. But what was sadness soon turned to silent rage.

"At least they couldn't smash my window," I joked, trying to break the silence.

"The gentlemen that did this will each be charged. We will also send some cleaners to help you with this mess," said Constable O'Riley.

"Thank you. Have you called my father?"

"Yes, we have a number of times, Miss Finch, but there has been no answer."

"Can you think of any reason why someone would want to do this to you, Anna?" asked the other officer in the room.

"There is no reason. They're just bullies," said Richard. "It's all her sister's doing. They all torment Anna because Charlotte tells them to."

"Do you believe this, Miss Finch?"

"Yes!"

"Is there anything else that your sister has done that we should know about?" asked O'Riley.

"Yes, last week she forced my hand into a blender…but Richard came just in time."

"Is this true?" she asked, turning to Richard.

"Yes, three other girls had hold of Anna. Charlotte had hold of her hand."

"What did you do when you came across this?"

"I yelled at Charlotte and immediately pulled the plug out of the wall. Threw it across the room and verbally abused the lot of them. I took Anna home, and she has been staying at my house ever since."

"Why didn't you come to us, Anna?"

But I didn't answer. I didn't know what to say. Every other time I was too afraid because of the consequences, but it was a little too late for that now. I didn't care anymore.

"Do you wish to give us a full statement down at the station?"

"Yes!"

Once at the station, I was taken into a separate room to be questioned. I was relieved to know that Richard was allowed by my side for comfort and support. I wasn't about to argue that he wasn't yet my boyfriend. As I waited for O'Riley to start, she set up a camera and a recording device. She said some important things before she asked me any questions.

"Please state your name and date of birth."

"My name is Anna Finch; I was born on the 6th of October 2009."

"Do you confirm that everything you are about to tell me is the complete and absolute truth?"

"Yes."

"To what relation is Charlotte Finch to yourself?"

"She is my older sister."

"Okay…Anna; on how many occasions has Charlotte tried to harm you in any way? May that be verbal, physical, psychological."

"Several. Too many to keep track of."

"Could you name a few of these and the people involved?"

"During school, she and her friends have mocked me, pushed me, bullied me, embarrassed me, stolen from me, and have even destroyed my belongings."

"Okay… could you please look into the camera and from each occasion tell me exactly what happened to you."

"Charlotte created flyers with embarrassing photos of me and threw them around school. I confronted her, got angry, and punched her in the nose. On another occasion, she stole my exam paper and wrote across it in permanent marker, something sensitive about our principal. I have a week's detention because of it. She put rotten food inside my locker. She created several Facebook pages that target me, so many of them belittling me and calling me names. She once killed these two baby birds that I rescued, got her friends to feed them to their dogs, and took photos. The photos were put inside my locker for me to find."

I told O'Riley everything my sister had done to me recently, stating them as I remembered them.

"She is close friends with the boys on the football team, the boys in her year; they once showered me with dirt clumps while I walked home from school. One of them intentionally threw a rock. They trashed my car I received for my birthday. They lured me to the football field, surrounded me, and started pushing me around. They pinned me to the ground and pretended to do things to me, which happened yesterday. I skipped school today because I was afraid of what they might do next. Richard and his friends stopped them. Somebody told the coach what they did, so their team was cut. I think they trashed my room because it's my fault their team was cancelled."

"Is that why you refused to tell the police what they had done to you? Because you were afraid, they might hurt you again?" O'Riley asked, her voice gentle but firm.

"Yes."

"Do you fear for your life, Miss Finch?"

"Yes! I do!"

"Since the last incident regarding the domestic dispute between Charlotte and yourself, has your sister approached you in a threatening manner? Or done anything to intimidate you?"

"She put makeup on her bruises to enhance them…and told everybody at school I bashed her. She's a compulsive liar."

"Has she tried to hurt you physically since then?"

"Yes, with the blender."

"What happened?"

"I came home from school with Richard; he was on the phone, so I went inside by myself. Charlotte's friends grabbed me from behind, three of them. They pushed me toward the blender while Charlotte held my arm. She tried to mess my hand up with the blender. But I screamed, and Richard ran inside."

"Could you not scream earlier? Perhaps when they grabbed you?"

"One of the girls had her hand over my mouth. I bit her so she would let go. I then screamed for Richard."

"Did you make this girl bleed?"

"I think so."

Constable O'Riley paused to write something down on her notepad. She then looked at me again before continuing.

"Were there any witnesses to these incidents?"

"Yes, mainly Richard."

"What did you see?" she asked him.

"I saw Charlotte with the flyers, and Anna forgot to mention that some boys on the football team pelted her with their footballs. She had bruises on her face. I was there when they surrounded her and pretended to do vulgar things to her. They pushed her and hit her. One of them actually punched her in the face when she tried to defend herself. My mates and I stopped it."

"Anything else?"

"As I said, I was there when Charlotte had Anna's hand in the blender. A few seconds later, and Anna could have sustained a serious injury. I wanted to bring Anna here," he paused, looking at me, "But she wouldn't let me."

"I remember something else," I interrupted, "But I have no evidence that it was her. Only a Facebook status."

"Continue."

"I was at the beach with Richard; he had to go, so I stayed for a while. I had a shower before catching the bus, but someone had taken all my clothes. I was left stranded and naked until a…friend helped me. I was told by a…friend that Charlotte had written a status on Facebook about there being a streaker at the beach that night. I thought it was a strange coincidence."

"What was the name of your friend that helped you?"

"Mirandah."

"Has she hurt you in any way?"

"She used to be friends with Charlotte, and yes, she helped put flyers up around school."

I felt bad for saying it, but it was the truth.

"You say she's not friends with Charlotte anymore? Does this mean she hasn't hurt you?"

"She has stopped," I interrupted, trying to defend her, "She apologised for what she had done and hasn't done anything since."

"What are the names of the people that continue to hurt you?"

"Michael Power, Dex Gunther, Abigail McGowan, Lauren Pennington, and Alyssa Almund. The only boys on the football team I know..."

"Derek Miles, Lewis Bentley, Roger Amell, Patrick Watson, Garrett Phillips, Marcus Knight, Paul Rowell, Rohan Peterson, Dustin Cox, Lucas Doherty, Adam Archman, Kyle Bennett, Rogan Sparks, and some other creep called Colin Murphy. Some of them boys are on that video posted on Facebook we came to you about earlier tonight."

"Yes, we have Lewis Bentley, Derek Miles and Colin Murphy in custody."

I wanted to ask about Colin Murphy and why he was no longer in gaol, but it was none of my business and I thought it rude, especially when I was being recorded.

"They will be charged for malicious damage, and then questioned for the assaults against Miss Finch," she continued.

"Will Charlotte be charged for any of this? When you find her?"

"Yes, she most certainly will. As will Abigail, Lauren, and Alyssa. But for now, is there anything else you wish to tell us?"

"No, I think I have given you everything."

"Will you come back in if you remember anything?"

"Yes."

Constable O'Riley nodded her head, turned off the recording devices, and stood from her chair.

"Thank you for coming down. I realize it's late, but these matters must be taken seriously. I'm sorry about your bedroom and your belongings. Do you have somewhere else you can stay until you can clean the mess up and get everything back to normal?"

"Yes, she's staying with me. I don't want her anywhere near Charlotte," Richard replied firmly.

"Yes, of course," said the officer, looking at me. "Lucky you have such a caring and generous boyfriend."

I was about to correct her, as Richard was not my boyfriend, but a smile spread across my face as I realized he had taken my hand in his.

O'Riley escorted us to the front of the station. As we walked to the front door, an officer walked through another. I caught a glimpse of Bentley sitting in a chair, his hands in cuffs and his head hung low. He looked incredibly sad. I frowned, unsure whether to feel sorry for him or not.

It was one in the morning by the time we finished at the station. Thomas, Luke, Sebastian, and Clara had gone home when we left my house, which was now surrounded by police tape. The cool night air brushed against my skin as we stepped outside. I was so happy to finally climb into bed, this time with Richard. The scent of his cologne was comforting, and his arms around me made me feel safe. He held me close all night, and for the first time in a long while, I felt a glimmer of hope.

14

That Sunday, I met up with Dr. Thorne at Murdoch's, a small healthy café in the main street of Bridge. The aroma of freshly brewed coffee and baked goods filled the air. I ordered a Chai Latte to go; eating something would take too long, and I didn't plan on staying long. I knew Lucia would find a way to piss me off, as usual.

"Hi Anna, it seems like forever since I've seen you last. How are you?" she asked, her tone overly cheerful.

Well, you seem to know every other time you see me, so how about you tell me. What do you know? Is what I felt like saying. She seemed to only show up after something drastic had happened to me. It was strange, almost as if she knew.

"I'm tired; I had quite a long and exhausting weekend. And I saw you last week, that's hardly forever."

"Well, it felt like it."

"Don't you have many other patients to fill out your time?"

"Oh, yes. But they're nothing like you."

"What is that supposed to mean?" I was suddenly angry.

"The people in your life are so fascinating."
I didn't know what to say or think. This woman was strange.

"Did something else happen at school that you want to talk about?"

"How about you start by telling me what you already know? You always seem to visit me after something has happened. It's as if my brain has you on speed-dial, though I'm highly unaware of the redial." Particularly because I don't like you.

"What a clever metaphor, Anna."

"Indeed, just like your 'be water when Charlotte's fire' metaphor," I mocked.

Dr. Thorne frowned, raising an eyebrow. "I understand that you had somewhat of a replay of the incident that happened in Jenson Park, or perhaps rendition is the word I'm looking for."
My stiff expression answered her query.

"You'd rather not talk about it, I see."

The waitperson sat our drinks on the table in front of us. I watched while Dr. Thorne took a sip of her hot coffee.

"I found a picture on a desk in detention; it was more of a doodle really. A comic."

"What did it say?"

"It was a picture of a spider web with a message written inside it, it was about my sister. I thought it was quite clever really, a kind of take on Charlotte's Web."

"What did it say?" she repeated.

"It said 'Charlotte's web of lies won't last forever,' or something like that. There was a tiny body dangling from this long line, it looked like a piece of rope. It was quite disturbing."

I paused as Dr. Thorne stared at me through squinted eyes.

"What happened with the police on Friday night?"

"Charlotte held a party at our house; she had told everybody it was my party. I have no idea why."

"Are you sure you don't have some idea?"

"To get me into trouble…"

Lucia sighed. "When are you going to realize that your sister isn't out to get you?"

"Then why else would she throw a party in my name? It's the only explanation of which I can think."

"I'm sure she has her reasons, Anna."

"Yeah, well I have mine," I said under my breath.

"What was that?"

"Nothing."

I bit my tongue. I wasn't about to tell her that I had had bad thoughts about my sister and wished she were dead. I don't even know why I thought it myself, so much had built up and I was so angry at her. I just wanted everything to stop. I decided to change the subject.

"I discovered the reason for why Charlotte tried to take my best friend and my boyfriend away from me," I started. "She wasn't trying to ruin my life by taking away the two people in the world that mean the most to me…"

"Oh?"

"She's jealous. Jealous that I have friends that I can look up to no matter what. They care about me, and they love me. And they're back in my life now…they finally realized that Charlotte is full of it. Her and her psychotic tactics. They're sick of her."

Dr. Thorne glared at me through squinted eyes. "And why do you think she's jealous, Anna?"

"Because she has nobody."

Because she's a cow and nobody wants to be her friend, I felt like saying.

"Don't you think that maybe Charlotte is lonely?"

"Yes, but it's not my fault. Why should it be my fault?"

"It is nobody's fault, Anna. Your sister is lonely; she doesn't have strong relationships like you do. Have you thought that maybe she tried to take your friends away because she wants you to herself? You are her sister after all; you should be the closest person to her."

"Not when she tries to kill me!"

"Despite the fact that Charlotte acts upon irrational thoughts, she still loves you."

"No, she doesn't. She wants me dead."

I want her dead!

"It's a cry for help, Anna. She doesn't really know or understand why she does these things. We have talked about this."

"I beg to differ, Dr. Thorne. She looked me in the eye that day she had the knife, she told me she had thought about ending me for so long. Does that sound like a loving sister to you?"

But there was no answer. It was as if she didn't believe me. She never seemed to believe me.

"Do you know why we aren't having this conversation at my house?"

But Lucia was silent; she sat and sipped her coffee as if waiting for me to continue.

"My sister tried to force my hand into a blender; she tried to make a smoothie with my fingers. She. Is. Insane!"

The psychologist raised an eyebrow and set her mug down on the table in front of us.

"Did you provoke her?"

"No!"

"Okay, settle down. We are in a public place remember?"

"I don't give a shit anymore. I don't know why you insist on seeing me when all you do is make me angry and blame me for Charlotte's actions. She has her own screwed-up mind, and she does as she pleases. I did not ask her to abandon me when I needed her the most; I did not ask her to threaten me or to attempt to kill me. I did not ask her to bully me day in and day out, with the rest of the school on her side. I did not ask her to embarrass me every moment she saw most opportune. I did not ask her to blame our mother's death on me, and I sure as hell never asked her to be my sister. Believe me; if I knew I was going to have this sort of life, I would have followed my mother to her grave."

"Well, I'm sorry you feel that way. I suppose you didn't ask David Hagan to attack you either…"

But before Lucia could finish that sentence, I had already slapped her hard across the face. She stared at me in substantial shock, holding a palm to her rosy cheek. She hadn't another word to say, and I was glad.

"I won't be seeing you again, Dr. Thorne."

I stood from my seat and stormed out of Murdoch's. The café's warm, inviting aroma did nothing to calm my rage. People stared at me in silence, but I just didn't care anymore. I never wanted to see that woman again, but I knew she would never give up. I decided to call the hospital; I needed to talk to the doctor who referred her to me. I pulled out my mobile and continued to walk down the street. I dialled the hospital.

"Hi, it's Anna Finch speaking. I was a patient of yours a few months ago."

"Please hold," said the nurse on the other end.

As I waited, I turned over my shoulder and glanced back at Lucia. She was still sitting in the chair, drinking her coffee.

"Anna Finch?"

"Yes."

"Intensive care unit…coma, is that right?"

"Yes."

"What can I do for you, darling?"

"Could you please put me in contact with my doctor? I'm unsure of his name…"

"He just got back from lunch. I'll put you straight through."

"Thank you."

"Not a problem, darling. I hope you're well!"

The nurse was a little more sympathetic than I expected, although I was in a coma for most of my stay at the hospital. It was strange; the only thing I really remembered was seeing Charlotte's disappointed expression when she realized that I was still alive. That's something I will never forget!

"Dr. Redwin."

"Hello, Doctor. It's Anna Finch here."

"Miss Finch, how are you?" He sounded relieved to hear my voice.

"I'm getting there. I'm calling to ask you a few questions about the therapist you referred me to."

"Strange, I have been trying to contact you about that. It seems I was given some misleading information about that woman, Ms Finch. You see, she isn't a psychologist at all. She gave a very convincing story in her paperwork, which gave me reason to believe that she would be perfect for you. But I was terribly wrong, Anna. She was never a doctor at Bowington Institute for the Mentally Ill; she was a patient."

She was a patient. A patient.

The words repeated in my mind, sending a sharp chill down my spine. I turned over my shoulder once more, but Lucia was gone. I glanced around the street, but she was nowhere to be seen.

"Dr. Redwin, are you busy right now?"

"As a matter of fact, I'm not; the last two days have been quiet around here. Only paperwork and a few check-ups but those can wait at least an hour. Would you like to discuss this in person?"

"Yes, I would actually."

"That's fine. Come right up. I'll see you in my office."

"Okay, see you soon."

I hung up the phone and walked briskly to a taxi rank. The chill down my spine would not subside. I became paranoid. I didn't know what this woman was capable of, and quite frankly, I was terrified; I had just slapped her across the face. A woman who proved to be mentally unstable and may well be subject to the unthinkable. She knew so much about me and what was going on when she wasn't around; it made me wonder if she had been stalking me.

The taxi ride felt like an eternity. The smell of worn leather and faint traces of air freshener filled the car. My mind raced with thoughts of what Dr. Thorne might do next. I found myself in Dr. Redwin's office in no more than fifteen minutes. Despite being indoors and supposedly safe, I couldn't shake the feeling of unease. The sterile smell of antiseptic and the soft hum of the air conditioning did little to calm my nerves. I was on edge, my heart pounding in my chest.

Dr. Redwin looked up from his desk as I entered, concern etched on his face. "Anna, please sit down. I'm so sorry about the confusion with Dr. Thorne."

I took a seat, my hands trembling slightly. "What do I do now? She knows so much about me. What if she tries to hurt me?"

"We'll take immediate steps to ensure your safety," Dr. Redwin assured me. "I have just contacted the authorities and made sure they're aware of the situation. Try to stay with someone you trust and avoid being alone."

I nodded, trying to absorb his words. The reality of the situation was overwhelming but knowing that steps were being taken to protect me provided a small measure of comfort.

"I'm glad I could meet with you on such short notice, Dr. Redwin."

"As am I, Miss Finch."

"Please call me Anna."

"I have been trying to contact you for a few days now. But it seems we have misplaced your correct mobile number, or there has been a mix up with your paperwork. We have tried your home phone, and I had even sent someone to your house, but it seems you're a difficult person to track down."

"Dr. Redwin, you would not believe the month I have had since I was discharged from hospital. All of which this woman knows about."

"Has she been seeing you?"

"Yes, often."

He frowned, and it was not altogether comforting. He looked worried.

"Does she know where you live?"

"Yes."

"Do you know where she may have found your address?"

"I assumed she was a legitimate doctor, I thought she may have been given it by the hospital. For visits...or sessions. But I don't understand how this could happen."

"She's very smart, Anna. We are not sure how she was able to hack into the system, but it is being looked into. The important thing is now that you never see her again."

"Is she dangerous?"

"It's possible. Did she mention any other patients to you?"

"Yes, the man who attacked me. She told me all about him."

"Yes, well psychologists are not allowed to disclose any form of information about their previous patients, or any other patients for that matter."

"I thought it was strange, but I also thought she was making relative points."

"Was there anything strange about her? Anything that made you think twice about seeing her? A gut feeling, so to speak."

"Yes, she kept trying to defend my sister. She would then compare Charlotte to the man that attacked me."

"How so?"

"She would say that they had their reasons for why they did things, that we shouldn't hate them because they act on irrational thoughts."

"Anything else that seemed strange to you?"

"Yes, she said…the people in my life are fascinating."

"When was the last time she saw you?"

"Just now…"

"Do you think she followed you?"

"I don't know."

The chills in my spine were back.

"Is there somebody that can pick you up from here and take you somewhere, preferably not to your house?"

"Yes, my…boyfriend. And I haven't been staying at my house anyway."

"Oh?"

"Charlotte has been…out of hand. Very hard to get along with."

"You've been fighting?"

"Like you wouldn't believe Dr. Redwin. She's very aggressive."

"Care to explain? We have time."

I paused for a moment. I didn't know where to start.

"She tried to kill me…"

Dr. Redwin frowned, sitting up in his chair straighter than usual.

"We had a fight over a cigarette, it was very physical. Until she got her hands on a kitchen knife."

"What did you do? Did she cut you?"

He blinked rapidly.

"No, I ran to my bedroom just in time. She tried to kick in my door...and then smashed my window. She said something about wanting to do it for a long time."

"Do what?" he asked, his face in expressive shock.

"End me...I suppose."

"Has she done this more than once? Or anything similar?"

"Yes, she tried to force my hand into a blender. With the help of her small group of friends."

"Did you inform the police?"

"Yes, she will be charged...but they can't find her."

"Did she run away?"

"Yes."

"Has she done this before? Ran away after a fight?"

"Yes, but she comes back after a while."

"And why do you think that is?"

"I'm not sure. So, she doesn't get into trouble?"

"When she's aggravated, have you tried to reason with her?"

"Yes, once."

"What happened?"

"She looked at me...like she was hurt. Like she was almost sad. But then it vanished."

"I see. I am not a mental health professional, but I have seen it enough. It seems your sister is suffering from some form of mental disorder. She needs help."

15

That Monday at school, I was assigned an additional day of detention for skipping class on Friday. The desk that once bore the drawing of a spider web was gone. In its place was a new desk, covered in a pattern that, upon closer inspection, revealed itself to be cursive writing repeated endlessly until no space remained.

"Do it. Do it. Do it. Do it. Do it. Do it," it read.

The words echoed in my mind, growing louder and louder as my eyes traced each one. I tried to decipher its meaning, but deep down, I already knew.

Someone wanted my sister dead, and they wanted me to do it.

At lunch, Richard had to leave town for a few days. He handed me a key to his house, but I was informed that the mess at my home had been cleaned and my bedroom restored to normal. I was eager to return. The cleaners mentioned that Charlotte had come home several times, acting as if nothing had happened, once again ignoring the charges. It was only a matter of time before the police arrested her.

"Those girls weren't at school today," Clara remarked.

"What girls?" I asked.

"You know… the blender."

"How do you know about that?"

"Are you kidding me? Charlotte brags about everything she does to you. It's no wonder people are starting to hate her."

"So why aren't they at school?" Kim inquired.

"I'd say they're at the police station, or their parents have grounded them," Clara speculated.

"The police know what happened?"

They both looked at me, waiting for a response. I sat in silence for a few seconds before nodding slowly.

"Good on you. It's about bloody time. People can't just do things like that and expect to get away with it."

"What about the footy boys?" Kim pressed.

"Bentley was at the police station the other night; they arrested him at the party. He looked pretty upset sitting there in handcuffs."

"Serves him right; he has done so much to you."

"Don't tell me you actually feel sorry for him now," Clara growled. "The mongrel deserves it!"

"I think Colin Murphy was put away again," Lucy interjected.

I frowned, surprised that she spoke up at all.

"Did he get done for drugs again?" Clara asked.

"Yep!"

"You girls love to gossip," Thomas said.

I had forgotten that the boys were sitting with us the whole time.

"He's not going to university anymore," Thomas continued. "His father is good mates with the headmaster. He pulled him out. He's joining the Navy instead."

"And you just said that we gossip," Clara laughed.

"How do you know this anyway?" I asked.

"Seb's dad and it's on Facebook."

"Bloody Facebook."

"Hey, all those pages about you have been taken down too," Kim said.

"How do you know?"

"Lucy and I and a bunch of girls from West have been monitoring it. We've been reporting them every single day and they're finally gone."

"Yeah, but it won't be long before there are new ones."

"Oh well, we'll just have to try harder."

It was nice of Kim to care so much. Then again, she would probably expect me to do the same if she were in my position.

As I sat in the cafeteria with my new group of old friends, my phone rang. It was Dr. Redwin.

"Hi Anna, how are you? It's Dr. Redwin."

"Hi, I'm well, thank you."

"I have some information on Dr. Th… Lucia. You may find it disturbing."

"Yes?"

"I'm not sure how to put this, but it seems that this woman has become quite obsessed with you. We assume Thorne formed an attachment to you when she visited you in the hospital before you woke from your coma. We are unsure why, but we believe it had something to do with David Hagan. You see, Anna, Lucia's birth name was Hagan. Thorne, she took from her late husband, who took his own life five years ago. We aren't sure if this was the cause of Lucia's behaviour, though her record demonstrates quite an alarming personality disorder from a young age."

"She was related to him?" was all I could manage; it was the only thought running through my mind.

"Yes, Anna. They were siblings. We have records indicating that Lucia bullied her brother from a young age. Despite being much older, his own mental state prevented him from seeking help. He once tried to escape from her, but she threatened to murder his wife and child. Lucia's attachment to David drove him to the point of punishing himself and others. There were a few domestic incidents reported…"

"Did you say she threatened to murder his family?" I whispered, standing from the table, and walking out of the cafeteria.

"Yes. Do you know something relevant to this?"

"Yes, she told me he murdered his own family."

"No, that is false. The only person this man ever killed was himself."

"Are you sure about that?"

"What are you suggesting? That David Hagan did murder his own family?"

"No, Dr. Redwin. I don't think David laid a single hand on his family. I think she did."

There was a long silence, and for a moment, I wondered if Dr. Redwin could get into serious trouble for sharing such information with me.

"The police are going to look further into this, but Anna, you must stay away from this woman from now on."

"I have no intention of going anywhere near her. Not when she could be guilty of murder and God knows what else."

"Good. Well, you will be hearing from me."

"Okay, goodbye."

I hung up the phone. Suddenly, it all made sense. Lucia was defending Charlotte; she was defending herself as I was relative to David. They were siblings, brother, and sister, and yet she beat him and bullied him until she drove him insane. He was a grown man, yet she intimidated him. He never got help because he was slow, but he must have known what she was doing was wrong. And now it was quite possible that Lucia not only murdered his family but David too. I had to stay away from this woman. She was more insane than my own sister. But since speaking with Dr. Redwin about Charlotte, I knew she needed help. And maybe she did feel bad for hurting me, and that's why she ran away. Unless she ran to avoid the police, to avoid prison because she didn't want to get caught. She's guilty and she knows it. She's bashed me, embarrassed me, threatened me, tried to kill me, and still plays the victim. She doesn't deserve an apology from me.

"Heads up loser!" shouted a voice.

As I looked up from my locker, a tomato flew toward my face, striking me squarely between the eyes. But it didn't end there. The football team stood metres down the corridor, holding lunch bins, and pelting rotten food at me. I hastily emptied my locker into my backpack and bolted. They chased me right out the gate and into the street until the principal intervened. Tears streamed down my face. I glanced back at the school to see my sister standing there with a smug expression, her arms folded. I was covered from head to toe in rotten food. And it was all her doing.

I turned and ran, not realizing where I was headed until I reached the lawn of my front yard. My heart ached, and the tears wouldn't stop. I sobbed uncontrollably. I walked through the door and headed straight for the shower. I stuffed my clothes into a plastic bag, threw my backpack on the floor, and stepped into the shower. I let the hot water wash away all remnants of food and grime. After washing my hair three times, I just stood beneath the water. I didn't move, I didn't speak, and I hardly blinked. I thought about everything Charlotte had done to me throughout our entire lives. I remembered her face when she realized I hadn't died—the disappointment in her eyes. Tears threatened again, my heart ached, and I suddenly couldn't feel my legs. I collapsed in the shower and cried. Deep sobs that took my breath away. My body shook. I clutched my legs and rocked back and forth on the shower floor, the water washing away my tears. I had never felt so alone.

That afternoon, Richard's mother dropped Douglas off. She pushed him through the front door as I told her I was busy, which wasn't entirely a lie; I busied myself in an attempt to clear my mind. But as I glanced at every photograph I put back on my wall, no shred of happiness stirred within me. I didn't even bother letting Douglas into my bedroom. I was numb to the outside world until my phone rang.

It was a private number, and for a second, I wasn't going to answer.

"Hello."

But there was no reply, just an eerie silence that seemed to drag on.

"Is anybody there?"

"Is she home?" came an unfamiliar voice. I couldn't tell if it was male or female.

"Excuse me?"

"Is she home? Have you done it yet?"

"Who is this?"

"Never mind that. Just answer my question."

"Not until you tell me who you are," I snapped.

But the line went dead. I cancelled the call and set my phone on my new dresser. Frowning, I stared at it for quite some time, as if expecting it to ring again. To my surprise, it did, only this time it was my father.

"Dad! Oh my god, how are you?"

"Anna, hey. Sorry, I can't talk long, darling; you wouldn't believe how busy I am with work. How is everything?"

"Good," I lied.

"I've received a few calls here, from the hospital and the police. Are you sure everything is, okay?"

"Yeah, Dad. There was some mix-up, but everything is fine now. Don't worry. When will you be home?"

"Not for a few days, I'm still out of town."

"Out of town? I thought you were at the office."

"I told Charlotte when I left that I'd be out of town for at least a week. Did she not tell you?"

"No, she didn't."

"Right. Okay. Is she treating you better?"

"Like you wouldn't believe," I lied again.

"Okay, well I have to go. I'll see you soon. Bye."

The line had died before I could say anything else. It was nice to hear his voice, even if only for a few seconds. The frustration of his constant work was a small price to pay compared to the alternative. When he wasn't working, he was drinking, and that was far worse. He seemed to forget he had a family, lost in his own world.

I tossed my garbage-tainted clothes into the bin and gathered my schoolwork and textbooks. As I threw my backpack against the dresser, my phone rang again.

"Hello."

"Is she home? Have you done it yet?"

"Who is this?"

"Is she still alive? Does the bitch still live?"

"Who?"

"Your whore of a sister that you complain about day in and day out…Charlotte."

Charlotte. Charlotte. Charlotte. The words echoed in my mind. I suddenly thought of the desk in detention, the drawing of the spider web and the scribbled words that read 'Do it.' This person wanted me to kill my sister. But who was this person?

"Is she home? Have you done it?"

"No!"

"Do it!"

"Why?"

"Because you're miserable because of that bitch, that's why. She makes your life hell. She torments you. She bullies you. She tried to take away people that meant the world to you, only to satisfy her own psychotic needs. Think of everything she has done to you in the past and in the present. Think of what she might do next. You have to stop her. It won't take much."

"She doesn't mean to hurt me," I whispered, but as I said the words, I wondered why I was defending her.

"She didn't care that you almost died. It's her fault you almost died anyway. She left you all alone, she may as well have dropped you off in the middle of that forest. It's her fault you were raped."

A chill trickled down my spine, and the hair on the back of my neck stood on end. It was the first time I had heard that word since that night in Jenson Park.

"How do you know that?"

"Well, Anna, everybody knows it. She laughed so hard she almost cried, isn't that, right? And that makes you sad, doesn't it?"

And it did. The stranger was right. The more I thought about it, the more it hurt. I remembered the look on Charlotte's face when my father found me in Jenson Park. I was cold and stiff, beaten and bruised, but there was no compassion or sorrow in her eyes, only disappointment.

"Don't cry, Anna. She's not worth your tears. She never was. She doesn't love you. She wishes you were dead. Just do it."

My eyes filled with tears and my heart ached. The lump in my throat grew thick. I didn't know this person, but I wasn't about to let them hear me cry. I cancelled the call and threw my phone across the room. As it thumped onto the floor, a *ping* resounded from it. I rolled my eyes and scrambled over to see the message, anticipating a text from Richard.

HEY ANNA, CAN WE TALK?

WHO IS THIS?

IT'S LEWIS. FROM SCHOOL.

I DON'T KNOW A LEWIS...

BENTLEY. LEWIS BENTLEY.

My stomach churned. What could he possibly want? Before I could discard my phone again, another message entered the thread.

I KNOW YOU DON'T WANT ANYTHING TO DO WITH ME.

I KNOW I DESERVE THAT. BUT I'M SORRY.

IM SORRY ABOUT EVERYTHING.

It continued, each new line entering the text thread. But I had no words to say. Bentley was the ringleader, in my eyes. The ringleader of the boys, anyway. While this was unexpected, I didn't like the feeling it gave me. I didn't trust him.

I DON'T TRUST YOU!! NOT AFTER EVERYTHING THAT YOU HAVE DONE TO ME!! GOODBYE!!!

ANNA. I KNOW. I AM SORRY. I AM SUCH A PRICK.

I WANT TO START OVER. I WANT TO BE FRIENDS.

DID MY SISTER PUT YOU UP TO THIS? IS THIS ANOTHER CRUEL GAME? ANOTHER SICK JOKE?

NO, ANNA. I SWEAR.

PROVE IT!!!!!!

HOW? WHAT CAN I DO TO SHOW YOU I AM TELLING THE TRUTH?

FIGURE IT OUT!!!!!!

I switched my phone off. I wasn't interested in anything else he had to say. He would either find a way to prove to me that he is sorry, or he wouldn't. Either way, I wasn't going to allow myself to be caught up in whatever game he and Charlotte had hatched together. I looked at the clock. 8:11pm, it read. It was still early, but I felt exhausted. I turned off my light and climbed into bed.

Not one hour later, I heard a soft tap on my window. Douglas lifted his head and growled. Lazily, I climbed out of bed and pushed back my curtain.

"Richard? What are you doing here?"

He shushed me with a gesture and beckoned me out my window. I obliged. We were several metres down the road before he said anything.

"I had a strange request tonight," started Richard, "But I have spent the last forty-five minutes listening to a very sad, sorry apology."

My brows furrowed. *What?*

"Hey. Anna," came a familiar, not so welcoming, voice.

I stared at Bentley, a little shocked. I said nothing.

"I tried to call you. Facetime, even. But you must have switched your phone off."

Richard brushed his arm against mine, reaching for my hand. It was warm.

"I owe you a pretty monstrous explanation. I am actually quite ashamed of myself. I am a Bentley. I was brought up with a straight moral compass. I have disgraced my entire family. My mum wont even look at me."

"So, she put you up to this?" I spat.

"No, Anna. Nobody put me up to this. This conversation, this apology, doesn't change the fact that my dad is shipping me off to the military as soon as I graduate."

"Then why are you here?" I interjected.

"Anna, let him explain. Please," Richard squeezed by hand.

Lewis let out a long sigh. His eyes drifted to the ground. His body language screamed discomfort. His shoulders heavy and tense with remorse.

"I never…meant…any of it. Charlotte had a hold over me. I felt like I didn't have a choice."

"You always have a choice."

"A few weeks ago, Charlotte and I were making out. You know how she is. I didn't really want to at first. You know, go any further than that."

Lewis shifted his body weight and let out another sigh.

"I am still a virgin, Anna. Charlotte agreed to help me out. I thought it was decent of her to offer. But it didn't work."

"What do you mean it didn't work?"

"I didn't work. It. Didn't. Work. I couldn't get it up. And I didn't know why at the time, but I think I do now. Anyway, that's beside the point. Charlotte laughed at me. She was so cruel about it. I couldn't face the shame. Not with what she had done to you."

Lewis looked pained. Tears pricked his eyes as he looked at me. His lip trembled. Richard reached out and offered a pat on the shoulder. But I didn't move. I didn't quite know what I was feeling.

"I couldn't bare to see her let my secret out in front of the entire school. Especially when that's not even the worst part," Bentley ran his hands through his hair in exasperation, as if the next string of words was so far out of reach.

"What is the worst part?" I asked, finally saying something.

"She laughed at me and called me a homosexual."

"I don't understand," I frowned, "How is that worse?"

"Because..." he hesitated, "I have come to realise that it is true. I just haven't told anybody...until now."

"Let me get this straight. You continued to be a dick to me, because you didn't want my sister to *out you* in front of the school?"

"I know that is selfish. And I am so sorry. But half the things I didn't even take part in."

"Like what? I saw you throw the football. And what about the dirt? The rocks?"

"Yeah. I know, Anna."

"You pretended to…rape me!" I spat.

My eyes filled with tears, blurring my vision. My chest felt constricted, my heart pounding against my ribcage as if it wanted to break free. Bentley slumped back against Richard's car and slid to the ground, his body trembling. He buried his face in his hands.

"I'm sorry," he sobbed, his voice cracking with each word. "I'm so, so sorry."

His shoulders shook with the force of his sobs, each one more desperate than the last. "I'm sorry. I'm sorry. I'm sorry," he repeated, his voice barely a whisper now, as if the weight of his guilt was crushing him.

"I can't do this," I breathed, the words escaping my lungs like a final, desperate plea.

It was too much. My sister had not only broken me, but she had also broken Lewis. Even though she never told anybody his secret, she had used it against him. She had manipulated him, and he obeyed out of fear of shaming his family. But his allegiance to Charlotte all this time was his undoing. His family did shame him. They expected better.

I turned to Richard and shook my head slowly. He needed to be there for Lewis, even though all I wanted was to be alone. I sprinted for home, my mind a whirlwind of anger and confusion.

I buried my face in my pillow and screamed, long, hard sobs wracking my body. There was no one in the world who could console me—not Richard, not Douglas. I thought about everything that had happened since I was discharged from the hospital. Every hurtful, cruel thing my sister had done to me, and the malicious things she continued to do. She knew she was hurting me; she saw my pain, yet she didn't stop. She would never stop.

I suddenly wished I had never woken from the coma; that no one had found me in Jenson Park, or that David Hagan had ended it all. It would have been less torment than enduring this relentless pain and sorrow. I pictured myself lying lifeless in Jenson Park, Charlotte collapsing in grief beside me. How it should be. But I knew it never would be. It could never be like that. I couldn't live in this world anymore. I couldn't keep cleaning up the same mess. I was exhausted.

My eyes drifted to my scrapbooking penknife on my desk. Only one thought consumed me.

16

And so there I was, staring at my wrist with a small razorblade pressed firmly against my skin. About to give Charlotte everything she ever wanted; my death, gift wrapped. I felt numb, hopeless, and utterly useless. I felt empty. I had nothing left. I wasn't afraid; I simply did not want to exist anymore. My life wasn't worth living. But if it's full of hatred, hostility, torment, and insane mutiny, what life is? I heard the door slam. Charlotte was home. I didn't bother hiding the penknife, she hasn't set foot in my bedroom to say hello in about ten years. I wasn't worried that she might find me here, cold. She would be left to clean up the mess. Explain to dad why I killed myself. Explain to my friends why I won't be coming to school. Explain to Richard why he can't marry me.

But it was that one thought that made me realise that what I was doing was not only sickening, but it was wrong. Why should I pay for anymore of Charlotte's mistakes? Why should I be the one to leave and not enjoy a life of happiness? Why should I hurt everybody I love for one ignorant girl that obviously needs help? Why should I give Charlotte the satisfaction?

Then don't.

I put the penknife on my bedside table, quietly let Douglas into my room and climbed into bed. My head pounded and I was exhausted from crying. I closed my eyes and drifted off to sleep.

I woke a few hours later to some mumbling that was coming from Charlotte's bedroom. I climbed out of bed and put my ear against the wall to listen.

"She's such a loser. I swear, I think I'm adopted. What's that? Oh, yeah, she's adopted," she laughed, "Did you hear what happened on the football field? Ha-ha. Yeah, so funny. I was watching from the science lab, she looked so pathetic, I couldn't stop laughing."

Bitch!

"Mirandah? Yeah, I don't know. We aren't friends anymore, obviously. I found out that she helped the little freak when I stole her clothes at the beach. So, I slept with that guy, what's his name? The one she's had a crush on forever. Yeah, him. She got really mad; it was so funny."

I couldn't believe the words I was hearing. Charlotte's voice dripped with pure, unrelenting malice. There was a long, tense pause, and I found myself straining to catch any hint of the conversation on the other end of the line, desperate to know who she was speaking to.

"Who that David guy? No, I didn't know him. I wish he had done a better job though if you know what I mean. Ha-ha. If I knew he was lurking around I would have paid him..."

My heart sank, but this time, no tears pricked my eyes. The well of sadness within me was slowly giving way to a rising tide of rage.

"Little creep looked at me with these sad puppy dog eyes. Ha-ha. I thought I was going to be sick when dad asked me to help move her. She already looked dead, why couldn't she already be dead? Let the coroner take care of her. I was so pissed when I was asked to go to the hospital. And when she got home, he babied her. Ugh, it made me sick."

So much about my sister that I had been trying to piece together suddenly became perfectly clear. She wasn't just a monster to me; she hurt others too, and she did so without a shred of remorse.

"Her car? Or my car? Oh, I'm not sure. The boys messed up her car. I'm pretty sure she did the same to mine. I told the police I knew nothing about either of them. Ha-ha. Stupid pigs, they know nothing. Did you know she's trying to get me charged?"

I repositioned my ear so I could hear better. Douglas glanced at me from the bed.

"Yeah, and the girls. But she'll pay for that in a few days. Ha-ha. They all hate her so much now. They're all like,

'Your sister is such a cow. Can't take a harmless joke. She won't be calling anybody when we screw her up bad,' and stuff like that. I don't know what they're going to do to her, but I wouldn't miss it. Ha-ha. Might tape it and post it on Facebook."

That's it.

I had reached my breaking point. Charlotte was still scheming against me, and the urge to storm into her bedroom was overwhelming. But I knew she'd twist the situation, claiming I was threatening her. So, I waited until she fell asleep again.

By the time an hour had rolled around, a strange sensation had begun to stir within me, something beyond my control. The stranger's voice echoed in my mind, urging me to silence my sister. My heart pounded as I wrestled with the thought. I didn't want to be her silencer; I just wanted to scare her. But the stranger's influence was relentless, pushing me closer to the edge. My hands trembled as I realized how far I might go.

Do it. Do it. Do it. The strangers voice demanded.

Your sister is not out to get you. Came Lucia's voice.

Yes, she is. Do it already.

She is lonely. She is sad. She needs help.

Kill her. Kill her NOW.

Everything came to an abrupt halt as an epiphany struck me unexpectedly. My mind was inundated with a torrent of thoughts, all converging simultaneously. The voices of the strangers and Lucia began to coalesce into a singular entity.

Was the stranger actually Lucia?

My skin crawled. Bile rose in my mouth. I wanted to scream. I didn't want to be like that woman. The woman that murdered her family and claimed innocence. I looked down at my trembling hands. *What have I become?*

I stood up from my bedroom floor and started pacing. I wanted to teach my sister a lesson. But I didn't want to go to prison; I didn't actually want to kill her. I wanted it all to stop. I looked to a cardboard sword hanging above my bookshelf. I had made it as a prop for a school play a few years ago. Not quite sure why I still hung onto it. Suddenly the answer dawned on me. I gathered my scrapbooking supplies, paper, and black duct tape. I cut out a cardboard pistol shape, layered it with paper for bulk, and wrapped it in black duct tape for a polished look. Adding details with a silver marker, I crafted a realistic looking pistol.

With a notepad and pen in one hand and a prop gun in the other, I moved from my bedroom to hers. I pushed the door open, and light from the hallway trickled into the room. She rubbed her eyes, confusion clouding her face. Without thinking, I hurled the notepad and pen at her and gripped the cardboard pistol with both hands, pointing it directly at her face. In the dim light, my prop looked frighteningly real.

She blinked rapidly.

"What the f…?"

"This is a loaded gun, Charlotte; I suggest you do as I say before *I* screw *you* up real bad."

Charlotte was so shocked she could say nothing, do nothing. She just froze. A tear trickled down her cheek.

"So, you shed a tear for your own life, but not your little sisters? Bit screwed up; don't you think?"

"I'm sorry, Anna. It's not…"

"Save it. It's far too late for apologies now."

"Anna please."

"No!"

I took a step into the room, my whole body shaking with fear and rage. Somewhere in the back of my mind someone was screaming, telling me to stop.

"Start writing, Charlotte."

She glanced at the notepad and then back at me.

"Write what?"

"Your suicide note."

Charlotte began sobbing uncontrollably. She slowing crawled out of bed and onto the floor.

"Please, Anna. I'm so sorry. Please don't make me do this," she pleaded at my feet.

"Get over there!" I shouted, kicking her away from me.

A part of me was shocked; this wasn't like me at all.

Charlotte clutched the pen in her hand and looked up at me with sad eyes. It reminded me of something she had just said not an hour ago.

"Dear…no, you're addressing it to everybody we know so just leave that part."

She sobbed.

"I Charlotte Finch am a scheming, conniving, backstabbing, psychotic bitch."

I watched as my sister wrote these words down on the notepad. I was surprised she was cooperating at all.

"All my life I have hurt my sister through my twisted torment and torture. I bully her, embarrass her, threaten her, hit her and have even tried to kill her. No human being deserves this treatment, and I realise that now I must pay."

Charlotte started convulsing as she reached the last word. Her sobbing became louder.

"Anna is such a kind, caring, beautiful person who never hurts anybody…"

Until now.

"She deserves to be happy. She will never know how sorry I truly am for making her life a living hell. So, I must leave. I'm sorry to everybody. But…I just can't live with myself any longer."

When she had finished, I reach out my hand to take the note. While pointing the prop gun to her face, I skimmed over the letter. I handed it back to her to sign.

"Sign it!"

Charlotte did what I ordered her to do and sat silently with her back against her bed. Her face was so full of sorrow and hurt.

"This isn't a funny joke," she whispered.

"What makes you think it's a joke?"

She looked at me, frowning.

"You like cruel games, don't you Charlotte?"

"Anna, what are you doing? Please, put the gun down. I said I'm sorry."

"And I told you it's far too late for apologies."

She burst into tears again and began begging at my feet. I shook her off again and pointed the prop gun to her head.

"Do you like Russian Roulette?"

"Anna, please."

"I'm going to ask you a question and when you do not answer correctly…or truthfully, I will pull the trigger."

She sobbed hard and crawled onto her bed, clutching a pillow close to her chest.

"Were you really going to let that blender slice up my fingers?"

"No," she sobbed.

"Click," I spoke loudly.

Charlotte gasped for air.

"Liar. Ok, next question," I said, "Were you going to pick me up from Jenson Park, like you said you were?"

"Yes."

"Did you wish the headlines had read 'teenager brutally raped AND murdered, instead? I wouldn't have been a problem for you anymore."

I paused. Holding the prop higher to her head.

"Click. Click. Click."

Charlotte frowned.

"Were you disappointed that I didn't die?"

"No."

"Click."

"It's getting closer Charlotte; you'd better start telling me the truth."

"I'm sorry, I'm sorry, I'm sorry..." she pleaded.

"Do you love me?"

"Of course I do, you're my sister..." she sobbed.

"Then explain why you torment me; explain why you bully me. Explain everything, because it doesn't make sense. Not if you love me like a normal sister."

"I can't…"

"Why?"

"Because I don't know why…"

She started shaking violently before she spoke again.

"I don't know why I do these things to you. I just do. I don't understand what goes on in my mind, and sometimes I hate myself for it because I love you. I need help. I don't want to be like this anymore. I want to be normal. I want Mum," she sobbed, gasping and drooling.

Her face was a wet mess. She rocked back and forth with her pillow, shaking her head and crying so hard she could barely breathe. I stepped away slowly, lowering the prop gun, but she didn't notice. I wasn't quite sure what exactly was going through her mind, or what had just happened. I had made several 'clicking' sounds with my mouth, however, Charlotte didn't seem to catch on that they were not real. That the pistol was not real.

A stark realisation washed over me.

Tears pricked my eyes, and I suddenly felt like the monster. How could I do this to my sister? She was extremely mentally ill. I walked to my bedroom and closed the door behind me, throwing the prop across the room.

Douglas lifted his sleepy little head and yawned. I dove into my pillows and cried just as hard as Charlotte, my body shaking violently.

I was the monster.

17

The next morning, I woke early to apologize to Charlotte. I couldn't believe what I had done to her. My stomach churned, and my head pounded. All the hatred and sorrow I had harboured for so long had morphed into guilt and confusion. I wished I could rewind last night, take it all back. Not just because of the overwhelming regret and shame, but because I had destroyed my sister. For once, I was the monster. It was hard to comprehend, having been the victim for so long, but I was one small 'click' away from pulling the prop trigger. My sister had believed I was going to murder her.

I let Douglas outside and made my way to Charlotte's bedroom.

"Hey, can I talk to you?" I said, pushing through the door.

The room was empty. An envelope lay on her pillow, my name printed across the front. I reached for it, tore it open, and read its contents. Tears pricked my eyes as I finally understood that Charlotte was just as sad as I had been. She didn't understand her own mind or why she made such foolish decisions. She was truly sorry for hurting me and admired my strength to keep going in life. She confessed to everything; all the conspiracies were true. She admitted to being jealous of Richard and Clara because she couldn't find strong friends she could rely on, or a boyfriend who wanted to stay longer than one night.

I was truly heartbroken when you were found in Jenson Park, it read. *I kick myself every day for leaving you there alone. I hate myself for drinking so much that I couldn't drive or even walk. I'm sorry that I passed out before I could get to you. I couldn't tell anybody because I was embarrassed; I was ashamed of myself for being the worst sister in existence. You deserve better. You always have.*

I skipped to the last sentence, a postscript.

In my wardrobe is a box of cards and presents for each birthday, Christmas, and Easter, accumulated over ten years. They're all addressed to you. Take them; they're yours.

I opened her wardrobe and there it was, a large plastic tub full of gifts, cards, and chocolates. I was stunned. I never knew Charlotte to be so generous, more so than I perhaps, as I hardly ever bought her anything. I plucked an envelope from the box and emptied it into my lap. It held a card and a fifty.

To my dearest little sister, I wish you a very happy birthday. I hope your special day is filled with love and happiness. The fifty is for that dress you've wanted for months. Go and buy it. Much love, Charlotte.

I plucked another envelope and opened it to find something similar. Another card, but this time with a twenty-dollar note. I took two more envelopes and emptied those as well; one contained only a card, the other another fifty. I reached for a gift and unwrapped it. To my surprise, it was an expensive bottle of perfume, my favourite fresh apple scent. I opened another to find a beautiful silver necklace and a pink summer dress that I had seen Charlotte buy, assuming she had bought it for herself. I didn't understand why she never gave these to me. She could have been a better sister, and she wanted to be.

The screeching sound of an ambulance siren filled my ears as it drove past our house, heading toward the off-ramp at the end of our street. Our street connected to one of the main highways out of town. There must have been an accident on the highway.

Suddenly, my phone rang.

"Dad!"

"Anna," he started, "your sister has been involved in a car accident. Can you meet me at the hospital?"

I breathed down the phone. He didn't need a reply from me; my silence and shock were enough. Did I do this? Did Charlotte try to take her own life on the road because of me? Why else would she write me a letter like that? So many thoughts plagued my mind. I couldn't think straight.

I walked outside for some fresh air. I was numb. I dropped to my knees, my phone falling to the ground. I sat there for a very long time, no thoughts passing through my mind. I just sat in silence, staring into nothing.

A familiar voice broke my silence. How long had I been sitting here?

"Anna," it was Richard, "Anna, what happened?"

"She tried to kill herself. We had a fight…"

Richard picked me up off the front lawn and took me inside. I walked to Charlotte's bedroom and looked to the mess of presents and letters. He followed my gaze and then looked at the disarray. He picked it up and started reading. I remembered the prop gun and came to my senses.

"When did she write these?"

"There's more than one?"

"Yeah, look…"

Richard lifted the first page of the notepad and beneath it was the note that I had forced Charlotte to write.

"Sounds like she really needs help. Hopefully she will get it now…well she will have to, now they know she's suicidal."

But was she? Or was it me who forced it on her? Did I give her the idea?

"It was me," I said beneath my breath, "I made her do it."

Richard frowned at me in confusion.

"I put a gun to her head last night. A prop gun. It wasn't real. It was only intended to scare her."

"Prop gun? What are you talking about?"

I dashed off to my bedroom, returning with the prop I had made out of cardboard and tape. Richard raised his eyebrows.

"She thought it was real. Scared the hell out of her."

"Anna, this is not your fault..." he started, but his ringtone interrupted him.

It was Mirandah. He put his phone on loudspeaker.

"Richard, did you find Anna?" Mirandah started.

"Yeah, we're both here. You're on loudspeaker." He spoke into the phone.

There was a soft sobbing and sniffles in the background, other people were with Mirandah. I looked up at Richard in alarm.

"Mirandah's mother was the paramedic on call last night," spoke Richard softly.

"They're all dead," came the whisper.

"Mirandah, what happened? Who? What does your mum know?" rushed Richard.

"They were playing chicken, like they always do. Miles' car and Watson's. They collided."

"What do you mean?" I asked.

"They took Miles' car out last night. Abi, Danielle, Bentley, Miles. That Colin kid. Alyssa, Doherty, Watson. And…Charlotte."

I felt a wave of heat rush over my body.

Bentley.

Suddenly, I couldn't feel my feet.

Charlotte.

My legs gave way, and I fell to the ground. My sister is dead. She's gone. But I wanted this, didn't I? Richard walked off down the hall, his voice a mumble, his words inaudible. I could feel the blood rushing, my heart thumping in my throat and ears. I didn't understand.

My phone pinged. It was a message from dad.

Get to the hospital now!

18

Dad sat in the sterile hospital waiting room, his hands trembling as he clutched his phone. The door opened, and a police officer walked in, his expression sombre.

"Mr. Finch?" the officer asked.

Dad nodded, standing up. I stood at his side.

"I'm Officer Harris. I need to inform you about the circumstances of the accident," he began, his voice steady but filled with gravity. "All the teenagers in the car were drinking and driving. It appears they lost control of the vehicle, which resulted in the crash. I'm so sorry."

I felt my knees buckle, the weight of the news crashing down on me like a tidal wave. It was true. My vision blurred with tears as I tried to steady myself. Beside me, I felt Dad's body begin to tremble uncontrollably, his arm brushing against mine. His silent sobs shook us both, a shared grief that was almost too much to bear. We stood side by side, clinging to each other in the sterile hospital waiting room.

"And Charlotte?" dad managed to ask, his voice barely a whisper.

"Your daughter was the only one who survived," Officer Harris continued gently.   "But she has sustained severe head injuries. The doctors are doing everything they can."

The words hung in the air, heavy and suffocating. My mind raced, trying to process the reality of the situation.

She's alive?

The church was filled with an overwhelming scent of white roses, their delicate petals scattered across the floor and draped over the caskets that lined the front of the room. Each casket bore a photograph of the departed, capturing moments of joy and life now painfully absent. The soft strains of Sarah McLachlan's, *Angel,* played in the background, its familiar melody weaving through the air and mingling with the quiet sobs of the mourners. The song swelled, its notes rising and falling like the waves of grief that washed over the congregation. In that moment, surrounded by the symbols of love and loss, the mourners found a fragile sense of unity, bound together by their shared sorrow and the memories of those they had lost.

Families and friends clung to each other, their faces etched with grief and disbelief. The weight of loss hung heavy in the air, almost tangible in its intensity. One of the girl's mothers knelt beside her casket, her fingers tracing the outline of her child's face in the photograph, tears streaming down her cheeks.

Alyssa.

Nearby, an elderly man stood stoically, his eyes fixed on the casket of his grandson, his shoulders shaking with silent sobs.

Lucas.

The minister's voice broke through the sorrow, "Today, we gather here to pay our final respects to each of these beautiful young souls that have lost their lives in such a tragedy."

I zoned out. It was hard to resonate with *beautiful souls*, when each of these people harmed me in one way or another. The minister continued to offer words of comfort and remembrance.

"…each a reminder of the fragility of existence."
The minister's steady tone could not mask the heartbreak that permeated the room. As he spoke, the parents, families, friends and classmates of each person's gaze shifted from one casket to the next, each representing a life cut tragically short.
Eight caskets lined up, side-by-side. The minister started naming each of them, breaking me from my numbness. Each name was followed by a momentous pause to give respect to the fallen.

"Danielle Chester."

"Abigail McGowan."

"Alyssa Almund."

"Patrick Watson."

"Lucas Doherty."

"Derek Miles."

"Colin Murphy."

"Lewis Bentley."

I looked at the last photograph. The weight of Lewis's reality hit me. I remembered the night he apologized, just several days ago. Even after everything he confessed to me, I couldn't give him an apology as I felt he didn't deserve it. *We all have a choice*; I had said to him. But I guess I didn't completely understand what he was going through, his truth being harboured as blackmail by my sister.

"Charlotte Finch, the only survivor in this tragic loss."

The minister's words pulled me from my thoughts again. I hadn't yet been to the hospital properly. I couldn't bring myself to see her like that. Guilt stabbed me in the side. It hurt. I was hurt.

After the funeral, Bentley's mother came over, sorrow filled her red, swollen eyes. Her smile was soft. I froze. I couldn't anticipate why she would walk over to me.

"Anna," she said, rubbing my arm in comfort, "Lewis told me everything."

My heart sank. My eyes filled with tears again. I felt like I was choking; my chest was so tight.

"I am so sorry," she said gently, pulling me in for an embrace.

She smelled like flowers and shampoo. Her body was warm, comforting. I didn't want to let go. Ever. I have never had this. The sorrow radiated through me as I so desperately wanted to hold onto that moment of comfort amidst the sea of grief. Bentley's mother held me tightly, her embrace a lifeline in the storm of my emotions. I could feel her own sorrow mingling with mine, a shared pain that somehow made the burden a little lighter.

As we stood there, wrapped in each other's arms, the reality of the loss settled over us like a heavy shroud. Danni and Lizzy's rendition of *Dancing in the sky*, played softly as people started filing out of the chapel. I remained rooted to the spot, unable to move, unable to let go of the only solace I had found.

Bentley's mother finally pulled back, her eyes searching mine. "You're not alone, Anna," she whispered, her voice trembling. "We'll get through this together."

"Mrs Bentley," I started, the words difficult to hear myself, "Why didn't he go home that night?"

Lewis's mother sighed heavily before she spoke.

"He did, Anna. He came home and told us both the entire truth. Joe didn't take it so well..." she hesitated, glancing over at her husband who was talking quietly to others, "He spoke so much cruelty to Lewis....and his...sexuality. But I embraced him with love. He is my son. How could I not love him unconditionally? I just wanted him to be happy!"

Tears flowed down her cheeks. She reached for a tissue to wipe them away.

"Lewis. He rushed out the door. I tried to stop him, but he climbed into that car so quickly, he was gone before I reached the other side of the front lawn."

I found no words. My heart broke. For her. For Lewis. He tried to make amends. He wanted to put every wrongdoing behind him. He wanted to make anew. But life had other plans, cruel and unyielding. The weight of his apologies and unfinished dreams pressed heavily on my chest. I could almost hear his voice, filled with regret and hope, echoing in my mind.

Lewis was burdened by his past yet strived for a better future. His efforts to right his wrongs were genuine, his desire to start afresh palpable. But now, all that remained were memories and the haunting realization that he would never get the chance to fully redeem himself.

As I stood there, the enormity of the loss washed over me. It wasn't just Lewis we had lost, but the promise of what he could have been. The future he had envisioned, the peace he had sought, all gone in an instant. My heart ached for the life he would never live, for the forgiveness he would never receive. From me.

I glanced at the photograph on his casket, his eyes staring back at me with a mixture of sadness and determination. It was as if he was silently asking for understanding, for the chance to be remembered not just for his mistakes, but for his efforts to overcome them. Tears blurred my vision, *I forgive you, Lewis. I just wish I had told you sooner.*

In that moment, surrounded by the overwhelming grief and the scent of white roses, I made a silent vow to carry his memory with me, to honour his struggle and his desire for redemption. It was the least I could do for a friend who had tried so hard to make things right

"This is not your fault, Anna. Okay? I need to know that you believe that." she said.

I nodded, unable to speak, my throat tight. She gave my arm one last squeeze before turning to leave, her steps slow and heavy with grief. I watched her go, feeling a strange mix of gratitude and sorrow.

The chapel was nearly empty now, the silence pressing in on me. I took a deep breath, trying to steady myself, but the weight of the loss was too much. *Is this what Lewis wanted? Did I drive him to do this? To not want to live anymore? Or was it truly an accident? Would we still be here if I had accepted his apology and made amends?* I felt so helpless. The weight of everything was too much.

I sank to my knees beside Lewis's casket, my fingers brushing its smooth wooden surface. "I'm sorry," I whispered, my voice breaking. "I'm so sorry."

The words hung in the air, a quiet echo of the pain that filled my heart. As the last notes of the song faded away, I closed my eyes, letting the tears fall freely. In that moment, surrounded by the symbols of love and loss, I allowed myself to grieve, to feel the full weight of the sorrow that had been building inside me.

For weeks, I sat by her bedside, hoping she would wake. She lay there, motionless and lifeless, almost as if she were dead. Doctor Redwin entered with a chart, delivering news to my father and me about the extent of Charlotte's injuries. The car accident had severely damaged most of her brain, but one area was particularly affected. He mentioned a complex medical term, explaining how the accident impacted the part of the brain responsible for memory. Charlotte's accident had imposed a profound memory loss, specifically affecting her ability to recall past memories.

"Charlotte has retrograde amnesia; it is a type of memory loss that affects the ability to recall information and experiences that were acquired before the traumatic brain injury. People with retrograde amnesia often struggle to remember events, facts, and personal experiences from before injury."

I looked at dad. Tears welled in his eyes.

"Interestingly, this type of amnesia usually follows Ribot's law, meaning that more recent memories are affected first, while older memories, especially those from childhood and adolescence, are often preserved. She may never remember anything that happened last night, but she may recall her childhood memories" said Dr. Redwin, "She may wake up and not understand why she's here. But she may also have no recollection of her entire life. Which means she won't know either of you. Charlotte has more or less hit the reset button on her life. I could say that she is very lucky to still be alive, but we still don't know if she will wake up at all."

I looked at dad when the doctor left; his eyes were red and swollen, his hair a mess. He was an absolute wreck, and I wondered if he looked similar when I was in hospital.

"I'm quitting my job," he said softly.

"Why?"

"You girls need me. Two comas in one year, first you and now Charlotte. I wish you girls would just get along."

"Dad, I'm sorry."

He took out his phone and dialled his work.

"Are you right here? I'll be back soon."

I nodded as he left the room.

I considered telling the truth, but I knew it would only bring trouble. Dad would blame me for putting ideas in her head. The only person who might appreciate my efforts was the stranger who kept urging me to murder my own sister. As I pondered this, I recalled something Dr. Redwin had mentioned a few weeks ago.

Lucia had murdered her brother's family before killing him, making it look like suicide. Dr. Redwin had filled me in on the details two weeks ago. She had vanished. Now a fugitive, I was relieved I would never have to see her again. I had had enough of dealing with people like that.

I took out my phone and erased my call log from the past year. Then, I logged into Facebook and scrolled through my newsfeed while waiting for Dad. "Nothing good ever comes from scrolling on this thing," I said under my breath. I decided to deactivate my Facebook page. I needed a break. Maybe I wouldn't reactivate it. The silence might be nice. Refreshing, even.

"Excuse me," said a croaky voice.

"Yes?" I replied, my eyes still glued to my phone.

"Where am I?"

My heart was pounding, my hands trembling as I sighed and looked up from my phone, expecting to see a nurse or a doctor. Instead, the only person in the room was Charlotte. I blinked rapidly, my breath catching in my throat. Stunned, I felt a rush of conflicting emotions—shock, disbelief, and an overwhelming sense of relief, mixed with the memories of all the torment and bullying from her. My legs felt weak, and I had to steady myself against the chair. I couldn't find any words. I just stared, my eyes filling with tears. She was awake. After all this time, she was finally awake.

I didn't know how to feel.

"Uhm, you're in a hospital."

"Why?"

"You had an accident."

And then she asked a question that I never thought I'd hear.

"Who are you?"

I stared at her for what seemed like forever. She didn't know who I was. Dr. Redwin had warned us that she might have no recollection of her life, or that I was her sister. Alternatively, she might remember everything from her past, including her childhood.

"I'm your sister," I started, "Anna. And you are Charlotte."

She smiled.

I smiled back, feeling the most heart-warming sensation I had ever experienced toward my sister. Her eyes were kind and gentle; it was as if she was a different person. I remembered my own time in a coma, hearing things even though I couldn't open my eyes. I wondered if Charlotte had heard anything while she was unconscious. *Did she really know who she was, or who I was?*

"So, you have no idea who you are or why you're here?" I asked.

She shook her head, her eyes wide with fear.

"You don't remember anything at all?"

Charlotte glanced out the window, as if in thought. Her gaze returned to mine.

"Why do I keep thinking of a thunderstorm?" Charlotte's voice was barely a whisper, her confusion palpable. "Every time I look at you, it's like I can hear the rain and feel the thunder booming inside my heart. But there's also warmth, and comfort. It's confusing."

I didn't know how to respond. *Of all things, this is what she remembers?*

"Do you know what it means?"

I could have told her everything—who she was, what she did, and how she had treated me all her life. I could have revealed the absolute truth, even about the prop gun and the real reason she was here. But I chose not to. *We all have a choice.*

Whether Charlotte was telling the truth or if she truly remembered me at all, I would never know. She would never tell me. It felt as though she was offering us both a second chance. She was a different person now, and I realized this was the beginning of the rest of our lives. Was it poetic justice? Or *enmity in retrograde?*